Ordinarily Sarah

Ordinarily Sarah

SARAH ELIZABETH ROSE

LitPrime Solutions
East Brunswick Office Evolution
1 Tower Center Boulevard, Ste 1510
East Brunswick, NJ 08816
www.litprime.com
Phone: 1-800-981-9893

Published by LitPrime Solutions: 01/22/2025

ISBN: 979-8-88703-448-5(sc)
ISBN: 979-8-88703-449-2(e)

Library of Congress Control Number: 2025900107

Contents

PART 4

For my daughter "Annie," and her 6
children . . .
And for all children everywhere who
suffer in silence . . .

While they wait for someone to come
for them . . .

This book was beyond difficult to write. Each page, every word, brought back painful memories. I lived the story over and over and over again in my head. And in between the memories and the writing of the pages, I had to quit many times, paralyzed with sorrow and grief. In order to begin again, I would place my daughter's face, and her children's faces, (at least what I thought their faces might look like), before me, and tell myself that they were real. And I would make myself listen to Annie's children crying out to me in my dreams, "Help us Grandma! Help us! Don't give up Grandma! Don't stop until you are done!" And I would listen to Annie's voice above her children's cries, whispering to me, "I love you mom. But I can't come home. I need to stay and protect the children."

During the writing of this book, I struggled with the people who did not believe me. I struggled with believing the story myself. I struggled with believing that God would ever help the children. And I struggled with believing in God. That was the worst struggle of all, questioning my belief in God.

But some of the people did believe my story. And today I wish to thank all those who believed. And all those who stood beside me during the writing of this strange tale, especially all who lived the story with me and through me … . Including my children, my grandchildren, my siblings, and my mother.

Today I also wish to thank the Publishing Team at Ambassador International, who put up with my tentativeness, my insecurities, and my inexperience, as I waded through the process of getting a book published for the first time: Tim, Anna, Hannah, and Sam. Most especially Sam. Sam believed my story from the moment he read through the first draft.

I also want to thank my dear friend and private investigator, "Ted," who worked so hard to help me get the children out. He wrote many of the emails included in this book, always keeping me in the loop, always coming up with new ideas to try, and always giving me encouragement with his lame jokes.

And I want to thank my dear friends Allen and Melissa (prayer warriors), Bill and Darlene, and Ed and Karen (all worship leaders), Chrystina (my hair dresser), Carol and Pamela (church office co-workers), Ken (my insurance man), Jan (my Silpada Jewelry person), Dave (my other insurance man), Claire and Diane and Ken and Laurel, and Rich and Linda, (fellow Bible Study partners and Mexican food lovers), Vicky (steadfast encourager and co-worker), and everyone else over the years from far and near who listened to my cries and believed that I had a story that needed to be told.

I want to thank my lawyer, (lawyer number 3), "James," who believed my story and did what he could to help me.

I want to thank "Grayson," fellow "whistleblower" and "amateur spy" who also tried to help me by making trips to the local police department with information about the strange religious group located next door to his office.

Thank you to my very young nine-year-old granddaughter who seriously lectured me one day: "Never ever give up, Grandma! Don't ever quit! Don't quit until you are done!"

Thank you to all of the faithful people who continually prayed for me and for my family over the years—whether they believed my story or not.

Most of all thank you to my husband, who lived through it with me, prayed for me, encouraged me, advised me, and steadfastly stayed by my side over the years—and who kept telling me that the story was real and that I was not unhinged at all. (Well, maybe a little.)

And finally, I give thanks and praise to God— Father, Son, and Holy Spirit—who always walked with me, even when I did not know it. To God, who always forgave me, even when I was angry at Him. To God, who always tried to comfort me, even when I questioned His very existence and stubbornly refused to be comforted. And to God, who always believed in me even when I told Him I did not want to believe in Him anymore!

—S.E.R

PART 1

Where is Day?
Where are all the people?
Where are all the calling birds?
Only darkness is here,
And cold winds blowing,
And hollowed out souls . . . Where is morning?
Where is noon?
Where is any time at all?
But only night remains,
And time stands still,
And nothing moves upon the earth . . .
Where is Day hidden?
Must we seek Her hiding place?
Must we push away the darkness?
Will not Day come soon?
Where is Day?

Prologue

The Dark Angel took away everything:
She took away my child,
She took away my grandchild,
She took away my work,
She took away my purpose for life,
She took away joy,
She took away tears that fall,
She took away sleep at night,
She took away peace at daybreak,
She took away my family,
She took away my family to be,
She took away memories,
She took away the present,
She took away color and light,
She took away laughter,
She took away pieces of my heart,
She took away slices of my soul,
She took away the world as I once knew it,
And she took away my courage to rebuild it.
Most terrible of all,
She almost took away my faith . . .
And she nearly,
took away God.

She works for The Enemy: for the Prince of Darkness. She is a Dark Angel. There are Others just like her. All of them are Destroyers. All of them work for the Prince of Darkness.

A Legion of Destroyers swooped down from the heavens on March 26, 1996, the Terrible Day the Sky Turned Black. It was the day that my daughter called to say that her relationship with us, her family, was finished. Done. Perhaps forever.

One of these Destroyers had come into our lives *years* before my daughter made that call, entering our lives as Counterfeit Light, appearing to be caring, loving, and wise. This Dark Angel was also beautiful to look at. In reality, she was a wolf disguised as a lamb. And we had unknowingly welcomed her into our home! She had eaten with us at our dining room table! My family had not recognized her for who she really was, and we were all taken in.

This Dark One had been stalking my family for at least three years. She had been seducing my daughter and her husband, promising them great things if they followed her. But she deceived them; and when the right moment came, she gave orders to my daughter and her husband to cut out their pasts. And they did . . . leaving their shattered families behind.

These Dark Ones are adept at hiding who they really are. They may hide unseen in our homes, behind smiling faces and false words. They may hide in our schools, behind teachers' desks. They may hide in our parks, sitting on benches while they watch for prey.

They may give speeches in our public buildings or flourish in our church pulpits. And as they pose as Counterfeit Light—they wait for orders from their Prince: orders to destroy. The Prince of Darkness wants our souls.

MARCH 26, 1996

My daughter, her husband, and their only child vanished the Day the Sky Turned Black. Their souls crumbled like dead moths. Their bodies were left hollow. Lifeless. Their eyes unseeing, their mouths closed.

Perhaps one day I will tell the story. But only when I am brave enough. For now, I must remain silent lest the telling of what I saw infuriates the Prince—lest the Prince send the Dark Ones after me.

Now I lay them down to sleep
I pray Thee Lord their souls to keep
And if they die before they wake
I pray Thee Lord their souls to take.

Chapter 1

*I saw Satan fall like lightning from
heaven (Luke 10:18b).*

Today, 20 years later, I am ready to tell my tale; I am ready. I am no longer afraid. The tale must be told.

MARCH 26, 1996

My daughter, Annie, called to tell me a change was about to happen in our lives. It was indeed a change—a major one, and nothing has been the same since. On that day, pain and sorrow entered the world I live in—forever. Reality in the world I live in changed forever.

I can still hear my daughter's words from that day—the last time I spoke with her. At first I thought she was playing a joke on me, but I quickly decided otherwise. Her words were frantic, hesitant, and choppy. She was crying, actually more like sobbing.

"Mom, I have something to tell you. This is bad.

This is really bad. I can't come to see you anymore. You need to repent."

I heard pain in her voice. Palpable pain. What in the world was she talking about? But then she told me I could come to see her if I called first. So that was good; I could hold on to that thought. Surely it wouldn't be so bad. She was merely upset with me about something. It would pass, and I would not spend any time worrying about this.

Knowing what I know now, after not being allowed to see her all these years, I believe there was someone with her that day—someone besides her husband—someone standing over her as she spoke to me on the phone. Someone giving her orders—someone telling her what to say. She had no options. She was already in too deep.

I believe my daughter had no clue where those words would take her after that last conversation with me, and neither did I.

After hanging up the phone, I continued sitting at the kitchen table while going over the conversation in my mind. What exactly had my daughter just said to me? What in the world had I done to anger her? What did she want me to repent of?

I didn't understand her words, but I told myself it would be ok. I could live with any arrangements, as long as I could see her and little Rory. No problem. I was just imagining things. Imagining the darkness gathering. Imagining my soul heaving great sobs.

However, deep inside, my gut was telling me

something was terribly wrong. The sky was filled with Darkness. My soul felt heavy. If I had only understood what was happening! But on that day, March 26, 1996, I had no idea I would not see my daughter, my son-in-law, or my little grandson again for years to come—perhaps ever. Maybe it was better that I did not know.

I decided during those first moments after that call that there was no real cause for alarm. There was nothing to fret over; I made myself believe that things would work out. I would call her later in the week and ask if I could come see her. Surely, whatever troubling thoughts she had on this day would disappear by week's end. Surely the skylights would return to their rightful places. And—if I couldn't believe things would work out, I would pretend that they would.

But the Darkness of Denial had taken me in. I would simply will my fears away. And when I spoke with my husband about her call, I told him it was all just a misunderstanding. Things would work out. They almost always did. With the passing of time, dark skies nearly always changed back to sunshine.

Today, years later, I know that at some level I had seen that phone call and everything that happened before and after coming. At another level, however, I had seen very little. I had made myself blind. My husband told me later he had seen the warning signs. He'd had a glimmer of something untoward forming and growing in our lives. He had seen the Darkness gather. I had not wanted to see it; I had made myself believe that all was well. I would pretend it . . . I was really good at pretending.

Looking back from the place where I am now, I can admit to myself that there had been many warning signs during the previous three or more years leading up to my daughter's phone call. And I know now that I chose to ignore what was happening. I chose to dismiss the truth. How foolish! Today, I see that all kinds of unusual and unearthly things were going on in my daughter's life, and in my life as well, preceding that phone call in March of 1996. But at the time, I chose to deny it. And I waited to take action until it was too late. Things like this did not happen to nice families like mine! But truth be told, we had *welcomed* something Dark into our home—something cunning and seductive.

The Darkness named Deceit came first. Then Denial. Others followed. They had many names. And each time a Dark One came, it descended from a high place. It spread its wings and swooped down like an owl looking for its prey, talons thrust out, sharp as razors. And each time a Dark One descended I wanted to flee to a place where Dark Ones did not exist—a place where the sky was bright—a place where there was more light than darkness. But I didn't know where that place was . . . besides, I also wanted to stay! I wanted to fight for my daughter's soul. I wanted to re-hang the lights in the sagging sky! I wanted to find the Dark One that stole my daughter's soul and grab it from its mouth!

But I neither fled nor stayed to fight. It was all just a dream after all. None of it was happening. None of it at all. I would wake up soon. All would be as it should be. My daughter was fine. I was fine. As soon as I woke up, the darkness would be gone . . .

But the dream would not end! The darkness would not end! And I dreamed I was a small brown sparrow, fluttering aimlessly through the dark sky, circling, looking for the Dark One that stole my daughter's soul. And I wondered why I had been spared from the owl's talons, sharp as razors. Why was my daughter taken? Why wasn't I taken instead? And why the madness of this dream? Why was I a sparrow?

And if I dreamed I was a bird, why not a hawk? Or an eagle? A small sparrow could do nothing but fly about and flap her wings. A small sparrow could not stop the Owl with talons sharp as razors or stop the Dark Ones. It could not put back the lights in the sagging sky. Not by herself. Where was help? I could not find help! No hawks. No eagles. No other sparrows! Where was help? And where was God? Did God not live in dreams?

And I begged God to come into my dream—to come help me, the small and unimportant sparrow that I was. And I asked God to give me big, powerful wings and talons, razor sharp, like the Owl . . . I needed to be bigger, stronger . . .

But I couldn't be sure that God heard me. And why ever would God listen to a sparrow anyway? Something so small and weak? And so I fled.

I unfolded my wings as easily as if I had always possessed them. And I began to climb. High! Higher! Higher still! Up into the air! Past the darkness. Past the broken sky. Past the talons, sharp as razors.

And I flew for hours, a night and a day, until I came upon a small dot of green in the distance. I flew closer . . . and the dot of green became bigger. And I saw that it was a garden—a garden filled with flowers, fruit trees, dragonflies and honeybees, and small birds of every color. And I wondered how this small dot of green had been spared, right in the middle of an ocean of darkness? And I wondered why I had been spared from the owl with razor-sharp talons? And I wondered why I was here, flying over this beautiful garden?

Suddenly my wings felt tired, heavy. Should I land in the beautiful garden? Could I rest there? Could I hide from the owl and the Dark Ones among the flowers, trees, and honeybees? But I had no choice. If I did not land in the garden, I would simply fall out of the sky with weariness and perhaps miss the beautiful garden and land in the Ocean of Darkness instead. I began my descent. And I wondered if God would be waiting for me there . . .

But I did not land in the garden. I woke up. The dream had ended. None of it was real. Not the dream. Not the owl with talons, sharp as razors. Not the Dark Ones. Not the sparrow. Not the beautiful garden. None of it. It was all just a horrible dream—a horrible mistake. None of it was true. And if I could not believe the dream had ended, I would pretend it.

Chapter 2

ONE OF THE STRANGE THINGS that happened a few years before March 1996 was the way in which Annie suddenly announced her wedding plans to me. It was early summer, 1993. I was very surprised with her announcement because I did not know she had been seeing anyone. As far as I knew, she had not been dating at all since the previous Fall when she had broken off her relationship with Bret, a young man she had been dating on and off for several years. I had really liked him and was disappointed when they broke up. Therefore, I was extremely surprised when she called me in early summer of 1993 and announced that not only had they gotten back together, but also that they were getting married in 3 months! Her exact words to me during the telephone conversation were, "I am getting married in 3 months! Come see me tomorrow and buy me a wedding dress!"Despite the suddenness of her announcement, I was very happy for her—actually for both of them. Annie needed some good news in her life. We all needed some good news. The year or so after graduating from high school had not been good for Annie. She didn't seem to have many friends. She was elusive. She had little contact with us. And she had not been doing well at the University. She eventually dropped out in January of 1993.

Surprisingly, after Annie dropped out of school, (and before she and Bret began dating again), she moved in with Bret's parents. This seemed strange to me, but however strange I thought this arrangement to be, I was very relieved that she would be living with them. Bret's parents were nice people. They liked her. And they would not expect any rent from her. What a blessing for Annie!

But Annie had other expenses to deal with, so we began helping her out financially. She was working at a mall during this time, so with her work there, help from Bret's parents, and help from us, it seemed she would be okay. Still, I knew this arrangement was just a stop-gap. What was she going to do with the rest of her life? But I made myself try to believe that things would work out. I did not want to think otherwise. Deep inside, however, I was worried. Why did she drop out of school? Why did she have so few friends? Why did she break up with Bret? When had they begun dating again? And why a wedding in 3 months' time?

Looking back, from where I am now, I can see that during the time *before* The Terrible Day The Sky Turned Dark, our lives were turbulent. It was a time at once filled with hope and also with hopelessness. It was a time at once filled with great joy and also with great sorrow. It was a time at once filled with glorious expectations and also with no expectations at all. It was a time filled with light and also a time with no light at all.

Today I realize that during this time before we saw the darkness, the world had begun to tilt . . . but no one noticed. During this time before we saw the darkness, the world had been struggling to right itself . . . but no one helped to right it. During this time before we saw the darkness, the world had begun to shift into periods of more darkness and less light. But no one felt the growing cold that came with less sun and less warmth. During this time before we saw the darkness, the world had cried out for help . . . but no one heard.

And when that Terrible Day arrived, on March 26, 1996, after 3 long years of fighting to stay upright, the world as we knew it could stand no longer. The world had emptied itself of its tears. The world was sitting in semi-darkness. The world had run out of time. The Dark Ones had been given their orders by the Prince of Darkness. And the Dark Ones easily pulled down the skylights and devoured lost souls. And the world—clothed in Darkness—fell on its side and broke apart. Just as Humpty Dumpty fell down and broke apart so long ago . . . and just as all the king's horses and all the king's men could not put Humpty back together again . . . all the king's horses and all the king's men could not put the world back together again. Only God could put the world back together. And no one could find God.

But in that time before that Terrible Day When The Sky Turned Dark, in early summer of 1993, Annie announced to me that she was getting married to Bret and that I needed to buy her a dress. And I told her I would come the next day, even though I was shocked by the news. My husband and I had not seen this wedding coming at all. Neither had Bret's parents. None of us knew they had gotten back together! None of us had the slightest clue.

The day after Annie called me and announced her impending marriage, I traveled to see her at her apartment, just as I had told her I would. And I was very excited at the thought of helping her pick out a wedding dress! But things didn't turn out the way I had envisioned. She was in a hurry. She found what she liked within 15 minutes—right off a rack. Done! I was a little disappointed that she did not want to look further, but the dress looked beautiful on her, even on her rail-thin body. When had she gotten so thin?

Annie wanted that dress! So of course, I bought it for her. She was extremely happy! And I was happy that she was happy. At the same time, I was a little wary—a gut feeling. Something was niggling at me in the back of my mind. Something strange. Something undefined. But I couldn't make it out. So I kept my feelings to myself. No sense in telling anyone about my concerns. There was nothing to be concerned about. I was merely imagining things.

A few weeks later, while I was visiting my daughter again, the wariness inside of me rose up like bile in my throat when I saw a Dark Shadow cross Annie's face as she explained to me the reason she needed to get married. Apparently, one of the elders of the church she and Bret had been attending had a vision about her and Bret. The vision? She "saw" Annie and Bret together—as man and wife—beginning in 3 months' time. This church elder told Annie and Bret the vision she had was a "prophesy," and had to be obeyed.

Thus the abrupt coming together of Annie and Bret, the sudden need for a wedding dress, and the sudden need for a wedding in 3 months' time! I couldn't help wondering if Annie had felt that Dark Shadow cross her face as she told me the story.

Well, it was all very strange indeed, but I told Annie I was happy she was marrying Bret. What else could I do? Tell her I was uncomfortable with her plans? Besides, I did like Bret and I felt they could make a go of it. So I said nothing about the elder's vision. Annie was 19. Bret was 22. They were both very young and determined. So I pushed my misgivings aside, and I kept silent. I chose to not think about the dark shadow I had seen on my daughter's face.

> *But there were also false prophets among the people, just as there will be false teachers among you. They will secretly introduce destructive heresies, even denying the sovereign Lord (2 Peter 2:1b).*

I didn't want to think about it. It just couldn't be. I would pretend it wasn't so.

My misgivings would not go away. And it was harder to keep those misgivings at bay as a steady current of strange things happened during the next few months—right before, during, and after their wedding day. But then again, I decided to keep all of my feelings to myself. I thought was merely imagining things, and I was simply a nervous mother-of-the bride. (I was totally unaware that a darkness named Deceit had entered my life. I certainly had no idea that the uncomfortable feelings I had were just the start of what was to come.) So I pushed aside any misgivings, and I was thrilled at the prospect of assisting Annie with all of the wedding preparations! I would help her with whatever she needed!

But it didn't work out that way. As the countdown to the wedding began, we learned that she wanted *only* dollars from us. Nothing else. She insisted that the church elder (the one who had the vision about their marriage) would take care of everything else. Okay, I could live with that, but I was very disappointed. Once again, that wary feeling flared in my gut. Who was this woman and why did she seem to have such influence over my daughter?

> *In their greed these teachers will exploit*
> *you with stories they have made up*
> *(2 Peter 2:3b).*

I didn't want to think about it. It just could not be.

The day of the wedding came quickly. I arrived early that morning to see if there were any last minute arrangements I could help with. As it turned out, Annie needed lots of help with lots of things. We spent the entire day running around town doing errands and picking up various items that were needed for the 7:00pm wedding and for the reception. By the time we were finished with everything, I was exhausted! The wedding ceremony was about to begin! (I couldn't help wondering why I had not been allowed to be a part of the planning and activities for the day from the beginning. It would have been so much easier!)

All was in readiness for the wedding by seven o'clock. However, the ceremony had taken a strange twist. My husband had originally been asked to walk Annie down the aisle (as Annie's biological father was unable to make it to the wedding). Al had been so excited to do this for Annie! He was even happy to put on a tux! Also, in the original plan, Annie's older sister, Kate, had been asked to be Annie's maid of honor. Kate was thrilled! But the thrill was short-lived, for both Al and Kate. As it turned out, just a day before the ceremony, they were informed that neither one of them would be *allowed* to take part in the ceremony. We were all shocked and dismayed! We begged the pastor to let them participate as planned, but he would not budge. And there were no explanations given. We were totally blind-sided! Especially Kate! I became suspicious that someone had put Annie up to this as

Annie was headstrong, but not cruel. I decided it was that church elder's doing, but I had no proof, so I said nothing and advised my family to also keep still. We just swallowed our feelings and put on smiles. After all, it was just one day in our life. However, I felt sick to my stomach throughout the entire ceremony. Something was terribly wrong.

> *Our struggle is not against flesh and blood, but against the rulers, against the authorities, against the powers of the dark world and against the spiritual forces of evil in the heavenly realms (Ephesians 6:12).*

But I did not want to think about it. It just could not be.

As it turned out, all the people who participated in the wedding ceremony were members of the little church they belonged to. I was so angry with them! But I just pushed my feelings down. We would get through this . . .

I have always believed that even in the darkest of places, there is always a light to be found—somewhere. That light came for all of us when Annie became pregnant. She became pregnant right away. I was thrilled! My first grandchild! Then there appeared another light. Amazingly, during the 9 months leading up to her baby's birth, my daughter and I became closer than we had ever been. (Annie had been headstrong from the moment she left my womb, and I was forever trying to find ways to connect with her.) Annie's pregnancy did just that. Her pregnancy was our connector; I was so grateful. I put the whole wedding thing out of my mind— totally dismissed it—and Annie and I never spoke of it. Neither did anyone else. It was better left unspoken. We were all so happy about the baby coming and had plenty of other things to do and talk about. Everything was fine. I was about to become a grandma!

Time passed quickly. Before I knew it, Annie had entered the last trimester of her pregnancy. I offered financial help to them to get things set up for their new baby and was happy to do it. I was also happy for Bret, as he was close to graduation from the University. He would finally be able to provide fully for his little family. He had to finish only one last semester.

Imagine my surprise when Bret suddenly announced to us that he was quitting school! Of course I said nothing. They were adults. They were entitled to make their own decisions. Bret merely said that he did not need to finish at the University because his church would teach him all he needed to know.

I remember thinking how naïve that comment was, but then again, he was young.

I thought he'd figure it out eventually—hopefully sooner rather than later. I refused to fully recognize the wary feeling in my gut. I convinced myself that things would turn out okay. I would pretend that all was well.

*Put on the full armor of God, so that when
the day of evil comes, you may be able to
stand your ground (Ephesians 6:13).*

But I would not think about it. It just could not be.

As time went on I began to recognize that something was changing in my family's relationship with Annie and Bret. Something was a bit off. In the beginning of their marriage, when Annie was newly pregnant, they visited us quite often in our home, which was about a 30-minute drive from where they lived.

Then, there came an abrupt change in their demeanor toward Al and me. They began giving us the cold shoulder as far as our church was concerned. They stopped taking Holy Communion. They would still come to the services, but they would leave when it was time for Communion. They never mentioned why they would not take Communion with us anymore, and I did not ask them about it. Again, we all focused on the baby that was soon-to-be born. At the same time I was perplexed by their behavior.

Something that did *not* change was that Annie and Bret continued to struggle financially. (Why in the world did he quit school?) Bret was working at a small business, but he did not make much. I began buying them groceries and other basic things they needed. And despite their growing lack of interest in our church, Annie and I grew closer. (Or at least that is what I thought). I often took her to her doctor appointments and then we would go out for lunch and some shopping afterwards. We would talk and talk and talk. Finally! Girl time! She was growing closer to her step-dad too. Al was exceedingly happy about that!

Annie and Bret's relationship with his parents also grew stronger. Suddenly Bret's parents offered to let them stay in a small wing of their home—*rent-free!* (The same space Annie had lived in before Annie and Bret got married.) Annie and Bret were ecstatic, as the apartment they were currently renting was too expensive for what Bret took home as pay. This would be a big boost for them financially. Soon all was ready. The birth was imminent! We could hardly wait!

In early summer of 1994, Annie went into labor. Al, myself, and Annie's sisters, Kate and Meredith, were with Annie and Bret throughout the labor. We told jokes. We laughed. We reminisced. My daughter was about to give birth! It was hard to take it all in! Finally, when Annie was nearly ready to deliver, Al and I, along with Kate and Meredith, left the room.

We stood in the hallway and waited. I loved Annie so much and I did not want her to be in pain. Every time she cried out, my soul cried out with her. Then, finally, Rory was here! My first grandson had arrived! When we went back into the room and saw him, my heart exploded with love. For the next 21 months, my daughter, little Rory, and I were inseparable. (All of my silences about varying oddities with our relationship with Annie and Bret had paid off—or so

I thought.) Annie and Rory ventured over to my house as often as they were able. When they came, they would spend the entire day. I would often go to their house also! We played with Rory. We napped with Rory. We took care of all of Rory's needs. I reveled in their presence. I loved them with a fierceness that I was not accustomed to.

During this time period, Al and I also became close to Bret's parents, Dan and Liz. After all, Annie, Bret, and Rory lived in the little wing in Dan and Liz's home. So when we visited Annie and her family, we also visited with Dan and Liz. Liz and I became very good friends, as close as two sisters. During that same 21-month period, however, there were times when things were not good at all. I tried not to think about those things. I just wanted to love my daughter and Bret and their son. I didn't want to think about anything complicated. I simply ignored many of the strange things that were occurring in their lives— and in ours. One of the strangest things occurred a few weeks after Rory's birth. Annie and Bret had a dedication service for little Rory in their church and did not invite any of the family to attend. On either side! None of the family even knew about the event until well after it occurred. Why hadn't Annie and Bret asked any of us to participate in the dedication? Or at the very least, ask us to be present! But there were no answers. No explanations. Nothing. Only silence.

As the weeks and months flew by, Annie and

Bret became more and more protective of little Rory. They would not leave him alone with anybody—not even for a moment. On one occasion, when Annie, her sister Kate, Rory, and I were at the mall, Kate wanted to wheel Rory around in his stroller. Annie said that was okay as long as Kate and Rory remained in view. At one point, however, Kate wheeled Rory just out of Annie's sight. Annie became hysterical! She ran down the department store aisle after Kate screaming, "My baby! My baby! Give me back my baby!" (Needless to say, many pairs of eyes were on us during this event!) But even though Annie's reaction seemed a little over the top, I did not say anything. I simply went down the store aisle and calmly tried to settle the situation. We left the store as quickly as possible. I felt mortified and so did Kate.

As Rory grew, his parents became even more protective of him. They would not allow him to play with certain toys, claiming they were evil. I bought him a book at a Christian bookstore and Annie threw it away, claiming that it was satanic. Rory began to spend many of his waking moments in "time out." Even a small infraction, such as looking at someone in the wrong way, would result in him being placed in "time out" for very long periods of time. Rory would sit quietly, almost motionless, wherever Annie put him, his eyes glazed over. He neither moved nor spoke. He did not make eye contact with anyone. This should have set off alarm bells inside of me.

But I pushed the bells aside so that their sound barely registered.

During the Christmas season of 1994, Annie and Bret decided to take a trip to see Annie's biological father. He had not yet seen Rory. They asked Kate to drive along with them, but at the last moment, however, they announced to Kate that she could not ride with them because she was a bad influence on little Rory. Kate was devastated. They told her she would need to drive in a separate car. So she did. Over 2,000 miles round trip. I tried to intervene, but to no avail. Annie and Bret were adamant. I was sick with sadness! But what could I do?

Once again, I could feel that something was terribly wrong. I felt as if my blood were being drained from me and that dark clouds were gathering. But I refused to look at the truth. The darkness of Denial was living in my house. Even though outwardly, Annie and Bret seemed fine for the most part, somewhere inside myself, I sensed the darkness was about to swallow us all up.

Looking back, I now know I was living in a fantasy world with my daughter and Rory. I could not face the truth. I told myself that Annie and I were fine. Everything was good. Everybody did strange things once in a while. Truth be told, I simply could not face the darkness that had invaded my life.

The following Christmas, 1995, Annie called me early in the morning to say that they would be late for Christmas dinner. She explained that they did not want to be in the house for any length of time with any of the extended family members. She also told me that no one would be allowed to touch Rory or any of his gifts when they came. They arrived—late in the afternoon—just when most everyone else was leaving. It was all so strange. But I did not say anything. I didn't want to upset anyone on Christmas. I simply made up excuses for their behavior, knowing full well that no one believed me. Maybe I was making up the excuses for myself. Did any of them see the Darkness swirling about? Did any of them sense that something was wrong?

Many other strange things happened in the time period between Christmas of 1995 and spring of 1996. I should have put it all together. I should have said something. But again, I did not. I did not do one single thing, except try to smooth over all of the strangeness. After all, I loved my time with Annie and little Rory. I did not want Annie to get angry with me and tell me that I could no longer see him. So I put my concern for my relationship with Annie and Rory over all of my other relationships—over my other two daughters, over my husband, and over my entire extended family. I sacrificed my time with the rest of the family so I could be with Annie and Rory as much as possible.

In reality, I let Annie and Bret control our lives. I let the darkness of Deceit and the darkness of Denial take over by pretending they did not exist. I let Deceit, Denial, and then Fear grow unchecked. I was being seduced by something very Dark.

As time went by, between Christmas 1995 and spring 1996, Annie got thinner and thinner and was exhausted all of the time. Besides taking care of her own responsibilities at home, she went to her church every day to clean. And she took Rory with her. I visited her one afternoon while she was cleaning the sanctuary. Little Rory was sitting on a high stool. Annie told me that he was in "time out" for misbehaving. He sat motionless, perched on top of the stool where he dared not move lest he fall off. Also, each day as soon as Bret got off work he would join Annie and Rory, and he, too, would help clean.

Then the three of them began to attend meetings at their church late at night—night after night. According to Annie, sometimes they stayed until 2:00 or 3:00 in the morning. They were all tired—all of the time.

As time went by and they became more and more tired, Annie and Bret became more and more harsh with Rory. He was forever sitting in a corner, on a chair, or on a stool—doing "time out." I was amazed at how he would just sit there—motionless, never uttering a peep. Just staring—but not seeing—straight ahead. It was not normal. No child under 2 could sit like that. But he did. And I never said a word about it. I was afraid that they would become angry with me for interfering. More and more, they found ways to control Rory—every word, every action. I continued to say nothing. Inside, however, I was sick. Something was so wrong, and I didn't know what to do. In the meantime, while all of this was going on, their church elder, the woman who had the vision about Annie and Bret, was now their "High Priestess," and was having more and more visions and making more and more prophesies—especially concerning marriages, divorces, and having babies. More and more couples in that church were getting married (or getting divorced) according to her visions and prophesies—and more and more children were being conceived and born into membership—according to her visions and prophesies. At the same time, I was becoming more and more alarmed about the situation and about the power this woman had over others. But I said nothing. I did not know what to say. I was afraid of her. Who was she?

A day came when Annie and Bret got an unlisted phone number. They gave me the number and instructed me to *not* give it to anyone. However, I did give it to my daughter Kate. Annie and Bret became furious with me, and they refused to talk to Kate when she tried to call them.

Between January and March of 1996, Annie and Bret rapidly rose in their church—from deacons, to elders, to "ordained" ministers. It all happened within a few months. The only training they had were the late night meetings and classes they had gone to. I wondered how they could have absorbed much of anything at 2:00 in the morning!

But despite the fact I found things to be very strange in their lives, Annie seemed happy. Tired, but happy. I did not understand what was happening in their lives, but the bottom line was that I still got to spend time with her and Rory. So I simply dismissed most of the strangeness from my mind. I dismissed the truth. If Annie was happy then I was happy—somewhat happy.

On top of all the strange things that happened in early 1996, Annie and Bret suddenly decided to move out of his parents' home. They had been living there for almost a year—rent-free—and the arrangement had helped them out immensely! But suddenly something changed. Now they would have to find an apartment, pay a deposit, and pay the first and last month's rent on it—all at once! I wondered how they would be able to afford all of that? They were barely getting by as it was! Even with no rent to pay!

But they did. Somehow they managed it all. And I couldn't help wondering if someone within their little church had bankrolled them so that they could. After all, it was another way that that little church, and that woman, could gain control of their lives. They moved out of Dan and Liz's home one day while Dan and Liz were at work. Annie and Bret did not inform them of their plans; they just moved out. And when Dan and Liz came home from work that day, Annie and Bret and little Rory, along with all of their belongings, were gone.

Annie had talked to me that day. She had been frantic. She told me that Dan and Liz and all of the other family members were evil and that they had to get out of there, fast—before they all got to Rory. And so they fled. Without a good-bye or a thank you for a full year's stay without having to pay any rent or utility costs. They just left.

My heart broke for Dan and Liz. For Annie and Bret. For little Rory. What was wrong with my daughter? She was becoming a stranger to me, as was Bret. And at that moment, I became truly afraid.

Even still, I clung to a bit of hope. My daughter still wanted to be with me. Apparently I was not evil. So we continued to see each other and do things together as if nothing had happened with Dan and Liz. We never talked about it. I simply continued to pretend that all was well—at least most of the time.

Then something else happened that was major. Annie, Rory, and I were out having lunch together, combined with a little bit of shopping. All of a sudden, Annie began rambling on and on about their evil pastor and that they had needed to get rid of him! Sister Jezebelle (Jeze), their "High Priestess," and some of the elders had pushed their pastor out— along with the church secretary and the church treasurer.

Sometime later I found out that after the pastor was forced out, Sister Jeze took over. She had wanted to buy the church building, but the bank would not give her the loan. Apparently Sister Jeze then became furious, took all of her followers (approximately 65 men, women, and children), and began to hold weekly services in a local hotel lobby. She declared it to be *her* church. And she appointed *herself*, as well as her husband Jeb, as head pastors.

Then things began to change rapidly between Annie, Bret, Al, and me. She asked me for Rory's crib (which I had been storing at our home), a word processor (which I had also been keeping for her), and a sewing machine (which belonged to me, but which I never used). Bret asked us if we would give them our minivan (since we were about to buy a new one). We said we would, and we gave it to them free and clear. They asked for some of our furniture. We had lots of extra furniture so we gave them what they needed. Then they asked for cash. Lots of it! They said they would pay it back, so we gave them what they wanted. We gave them all they asked for and more: co-signed loans and bought them clothes, groceries, household appliances, and toys and books for Rory. We even gave them our piano! Why? Because we thought that is what parents did when their grown children struggled. We thought we were helping them to get a good start in life. Never mind all the strange things going on in their lives!

But deep inside, I was terrified. If we did not give them what they wanted, would they take Rory away from us? But why in the world was I thinking like that? Had a part of me stumbled onto the truth? Had I finally glimpsed the face of the darkness?

So we emptied our house and our hearts and believed that all would be okay. But after they got everything they wanted, they took Rory away from us anyway. Annie made that fateful phone call on March 26, 1996, and they left us.

They left us all—mothers, fathers, grandparents, uncles, aunts, sisters, brothers, and cousins—all of us. And none of us has had contact with them since. The day my daughter called and told me she could no longer see me was The Terrible Day the Sky Turned Dark, the day the stars, moon, and sun came down. It was the day the earth shook. It was the day the Dark Ones came, like Owls, with talons, razor sharp, fulfilling their orders from the Prince of Darkness. It was the day the world tilted on its axis and broke apart . . . just like Humpty Dumpty. And none of the king's horses and none of the king's men have been able to put the world back together again . . . to put our lives back together again.

What a fool I had been! I no longer knew my daughter. The daughter I knew and loved was gone. The daughter I knew and loved had become a complete stranger. I had been living in a fantasy world for the past 3 years. Nothing that I had believed to be real was real.

And where in the world was God? He appeared to be nowhere! And I wondered if it was I who had disappeared from God? And was it I who had refused to listen to Him? Had I refused to heed God's warnings? In my blindness and my world of make-believe had I refused to see either the darkness—or—God?

> *A voice was heard in Ramah,*
> *Wailing and loud lamentation,*
> *Rachel weeping for her children;*
> *She refused to be consoled,*
> *Because they were no more.*
> *—Jeremiah 31:15*

But I still did not want to hear it. It just couldn't be. And on That Terrible Day, when darkness flooded my world, I felt as small as a sparrow as I began my search for God.

Chapter 3

A FEW WEEKS AFTER ANNIE and Bret cut off all ties with their family members, an unthinkable event took place: an event I believed was somehow connected to Annie and Bret. Sweet Maria, a young college student and another child belonging to Dan and Liz, took her life. She hung herself in her apartment. Her sister, who was living with her at the time, found her. I can't even begin to imagine the horror of one sister finding another sister hanging in the air—dead.

Maria had kept a journal of sorts. Her writings showed clearly that she had been unhappy for a long time. She wrote about a rape she had endured. She wrote about her rapist who had recently been released from jail. She wrote about her fear that her rapist would come after her again. She wrote that both of her brothers (Bret and Ray) had scolded her right after the rape had occurred and had told her that the rape had been her fault—that she had asked for it.

How could her brothers have been so cruel? Had they already been under the influence of Sister Jezebelle when they made that statement to Maria? We all thought that Bret and Ray, both sons of Dan, and Liz and both members of what we all began to refer to as "That Group," would attend Maria's funeral. And we hoped that, through the tragedy, perhaps the family would reconcile. Wrong on both accounts. The brothers refused to attend Maria's funeral. Then when Liz tried to visit with them at their apartments, they sent her away after telling her that Maria was in hell.

I attended the funeral service with my husband and my daughters Kate and Meredith. It was an incredibly sad funeral. How could this have happened? Maria was so beautiful and so smart—she could have had a wonderful life. None of us could understand why her brothers would not attend her funeral. And why would they say to their parents that Maria was in hell?

After the service, Al, Kate, Meredith, and I decided to go over to Annie and Bret's apartment. Surely they would not send *us* away. We pulled in the parking lot and sat for a moment gathering our thoughts. Al and Kate decided to stay in the car and wait until we knew if they would invite us in. Would they *not* invite us in? How could that idea even be a possibility? Meredith and I each took a deep breath, got out of the car, and began walking toward the apartment building. Once inside we walked up a flight of stairs and scooted through a short, narrow hallway—right to their door. I knocked. No response. I knocked again. Louder. This time Bret opened the door, but just a crack. He told us, "Go away, we have nothing to say." I begged him to let us in. He would not. Was this the Bret I knew? His face looked different to me—hard, dark, twisted. He did not look like or sound like the Bret we knew and loved. Then he told us to "Go away, or I will call the police!" Hurt and confused, I began shouting at him. "I want to see my daughter! She is my daughter!" And once more he told us to leave or he would call the police.

We left. I was in shock! Broken-hearted. I will never forget what I saw in his eyes—fury and hatred. What in the world had just happened? What had we done to earn such wrath? Did my daughter hate us too? Would they teach little Rory to hate us?

For at least a month after Maria's funeral I felt paralyzed. I could barely function at home or at work. I did not want to talk to anyone. Who would believe that my daughter and son-in-law would threaten us with a phone call to the police if we did not leave their apartment building? No one! I was convinced that if anything, other people would think that we must have done something horrible. Why else would a daughter leave her family? We were in an impossible situation. Where could we go for help?

Feeling spiritually exhausted, we prayed, "To whom shall we go, Lord? We had thought we could wish it all away. Pretend it wasn't happening. Now we are lost! Now we sit in darkness! Come to us Lord! Do not turn Your Face from us!"

> *Lost in the night doth the heathen yet*
> *languish,*
> *Longing for morning the darkness to*
> *vanquish,*

Plaintively heaving a sigh full of
anguish: Will not day come soon?
Will not day come soon?
Must he be vainly awaiting the morrow?
Shall we who have it no light let him
borrow?
Giving no heed to his burden of sorrow:
Will you help us soon?
Will you help us soon?
—from Lost in the Night, a Finnish folk
song

And suddenly we found ourselves in the time *after*. The Time After that Terrible Day. And it was a time to build a new world that we could live in. We did not need a big world. But we needed a world big enough. We did not need a world full of joy. But we needed a world with joy enough. And so we built it. And we made it work. It was also better than living in a world only with sadness and fear, and owl-like creatures with stretched out talons, razor sharp.

It was during this time after that a part of me turned hard, unfeeling, and aloof. I continued to search for God during this time after—but God was nowhere to be found. Nowhere at all. And I began to feel angry with God.

I didn't like the anger I felt. I didn't like the hard, unfeeling part of me that was growing inside. I felt shame. And I was afraid others might see this part of me and be revulsed. So I hid my anger: I pushed it down deep into my soul.

About a month after Maria's funeral, during the time after, it came to me that an old friend of mine, named Linae, might be able to help me—help us—in this terrible situation we were in with Annie. Linae had become a social worker and I knew she would not judge me or what I had to say. She would be professional about our predicament. She would also be a compassionate friend. She knew me well enough to know that I would not make up something like this. Nor would she believe that I would ever do something so horrible as to cause this situation—that I would cause Annie to leave us!

I called her and she listened intently. Then she gave me the name of a relative of hers who was a Christian counselor. She said he might understand our dilemma because he had some experience working with strange, cult-like groups. Strange cult-like groups? Was that it? Was my daughter caught up in a cult? Was "That Group" a cult?

Within twenty-four hours, I called Grayson (the counselor that my friend Linae had suggested). I told him briefly what we were experiencing with our daughter and asked if I could make an appointment with him. He said he would see me. I then called Dan and Liz to ask them if they would come to see Grayson with Al and me. They said they would. They asked if another couple, John and Leah, could also come, as That Group had also victimized them. I said sure.

In early May of 1996, we had our first meeting with Grayson. It was difficult to seat all of us in Grayson's small office, but we made it work. We introduced ourselves and then we told him everything we knew about this strange little group that our grown children were involved in. Part way through our discussion, I had a vision and I saw myself disappearing from my chair! I had unfolded a pair of wings and flown to the ceiling! I was now looking at all of them from above . . . but I couldn't hear what they were saying. And I needed to hear what they were saying. So I made myself come back down to my chair. Wings all folded in and invisible. How very odd. All of it. All of us. Here! On this day. At this place in time. Talking to this man!

First of all, we learned that John and Leah had, at one time, belonged to the little church where Annie and Bret had been married—before the pastor and his staff had been run off. John and Leah told us that they had left the church because they felt they had been treated very poorly and because they had witnessed some troubling incidents. They spoke of church leaders who inflicted punishments on other members who were not living up to the congregation's standards. They also spoke of a particularly large, burly man who carried a gun in his boot at all times. He was the "church bouncer" so-to-speak, and monitored all people coming and going into the building. Dan and Liz related that one time they had visited the church and the man with the gun in his boot had followed Dan everywhere, even into the men's restroom! Dan said he had felt very intimidated by the big man and that the big man had been menacing!

Then John and Leah spoke of large sums of money collected in the offering plates at each service: extremely large sums for such a small congregation of 100 or less people! They expressed that they did not know where all of the money was coming from.

Next John and Leah explained that the church pastor, the church treasurer, and the church secretary were suddenly fired and pushed out by a woman named Jezebelle (coinciding with the story Annie had told me when Annie was still talking to me).

Finally John and Leah shared that shortly after the staff was run-off, Jeze took about sixty-five members and left with them to begin a new church. Our daughter Annie, two of Liz and Dan's sons (Bret and Ray), and Ray's wife Theresa all left with Jeze, as did John and Leah's son, Stan and his family. The big man with the gun also left with Jeze, along with about 50 others. (This information verified what we already knew.)

We met with Grayson for quite a while that day—at least an hour or so. Then we decided we would meet again soon. For now we all needed some time to think about what had been discussed. It would take some time to sort it all out.

Al and I left Grayson's office with a feeling of hope. He had been listening to us! He had believed our story! He was willing to help! We left thinking that Grayson might be able to mend our dark and broken sky. But we weren't sure he could mend our broken souls. Could all the king's horses and all the king's men put us back together again? Was there any hope for us at all? Or was I just pretending again?

After meeting with Grayson, I felt somewhat better, less paralyzed. I actually felt a bit of energy. And of all things, I began to entertain the idea of doing something different for our home! Perhaps a good spring cleaning? Perhaps some redecorating? Something to make our home look more cheerful—maybe a vase of pretty flowers?

My feeling of well-being didn't last long, however. I had thought I might start with our bedroom—perhaps purchase some new sheets and a new bedspread and curtains. But as I looked around our bedroom, a shadow crossed before my eyes and I thought, "What difference do new sheets, a new bedspread, and new curtains make in my life? What difference does anything make when my daughter, her husband, and little Rory are gone? Gone. Dead. Not physically dead, but perhaps lost forever. What difference does anything make? Anything at all? Nothing matters except getting them back." And suddenly the small amount of hope and energy I had gleaned from our meeting with Grayson vanished. And the hope that I had momentarily entertained turned into anger. I felt angry especially with Bret. How had he gotten my daughter and their little son into this mess? How was it that he had been acting so cruelly towards us—after all we had done for him—for them?

The Bret I had known and loved existed no more. And I wondered if he had been playing us all along? Had I been such a poor judge of character? Had someone plunged him into the darkness of another life? And if so, who? Who had flipped the switch? What had happened to him on That Terrible Day? But I knew. The Dark Ones had come for him. And they had taken his soul.

During this time after, I began having nightmares. The dreams were frightening, intense. I believed them to be messages from the other world—the Dark World—where no real light existed—only counterfeit light. It was the Dark World where my daughter and her family now lived. I was sure that these messages were from the Dark Ones. The messages were hateful, accusing, threatening. The messages lay heavily upon me.

All the better for the Dark Ones. They wanted to make me feel uncomfortable. They wanted to make me feel heavy with sadness. And they wanted me to stay put. They did not want me to seek out others who had survived That Terrible Day! They did not want the survivors to share their stories! They wanted to destroy me, wings and all. But why? I was insignificant and weak—either as myself, or as my imaginary sparrow. Why did they want to destroy me? Why was I a threat to them? What could I possibly do to hurt them? I was small and unimportant. And again I asked, why was I spared?

On May 14, 1996, I met a young man by the name

of David. Liz and Dan introduced him to Al and me. He had been a former friend of both Bret and Ray. David had also been a member of the original congregation they had all belonged to before the staff was run off and before the members split into two groups and Jeze left with her group and elevated herself to the rank of High Priestess. David had sung at Annie and Bret's wedding! But David had been cut off, too.

We talked to David for quite a while about The Group our grown children were involved in. And then, for some reason, I found myself telling him about two disturbing dreams I had the night before concerning Annie. They were frightening dreams! Vivid. Detailed.

In the first dream I found myself looking at a very pregnant woman. The woman was Annie. Annie's abdomen was transparent so I could see the baby inside of her. The child was beautiful. His eyes were bright and alert. He was straining to get out but could not. A tight veil of transparent flesh imprisoned him. Suddenly the child was out of the womb. Just like that! I found myself cleaning him up. He was perfect. Happy. Free of the flesh that had held him so tightly. Then Annie told me that the child had to return to her womb, but the child did not want to go back. She insisted, so I put the child back. Then her womb changed from transparent to solid and I could no longer see the baby. Suddenly sharp needles sprung up from Annie's womb. I could no longer touch it or get near to it. I felt a great sadness.

In the second dream I found myself walking outside at night near a thick forest. It was very dark. The stars and moon gave out little light. I was walking with a young woman, my daughter, Annie. We walked hand-in-hand. She was clinging to me tightly, frightened, because she had seen a large dragon-like creature, 20-30 feet high, flying in the air. It had emerged from a lake behind her house. She believed that it wanted to hunt her down and kill her. I told her to stand firm and to tell the dragon to flee from her. I did not know what else to tell her. I did not know how to help her. The world she lived in was so different from the one I lived in. I feared for her life. I felt totally helpless . . .

Sometime after I had spoken to David about those disturbing dreams, Al and I met with Grayson again. It was a lifeless meeting. My words were lifeless. I was lifeless. It all seemed to be a futile exercise. Grayson tried to be reassuring and comforting, and told me God would prevail. I wished I could have believed him. I wished I could have believed that God could help us, but I had grave doubts. God was still nowhere to be found!

Something was unearthly about all of this. A Dark Force felt near. I could feel it breathing down the back of my neck. And I didn't know how to make it go away. I didn't know how to stop it from growing. Our lives were broken, and I didn't know how to fix them. I didn't know how to put our lives back together again. I felt sure that no one could help us. Not all the king's horses and all the king's men. Not even God.

I felt abandoned by God. I had prayed to God but He had not heard my prayers. Had I waited too long to ask God for help? Was that it? Had I asked too late? Was I beyond being forgiven, then?

> *God did not send his Son into the world to condemn the world, but to save the world through him (John 3:17).*

> *Does that include me, God? Can You save me too? Can You save my daughter? Her husband? Their child?*

Grayson called later in the week to cancel our phone consult. I was disappointed, but I am disappointed most of the time. My life has become a nightmare. Even the new world we have built for ourselves is a nightmare most of the time. I feel lost—swallowed up by sorrow. I don't want to get up in the mornings and go to work. I don't want to see anybody, talk to anybody, or listen to anybody. I don't know what to do.

Do not turn your ear from me, God! Annie, her husband, and little Rory are gone from my life! They have all vanished off the face of the earth. What must that little boy think? Does he believe that his Grandma has left him forever? I want to hold him, God. I want to rock him. I want to see him smile. Hear him giggle. I want to hear him say, "Gamma!" What benefit can possibly come from all of this, God? Do I have something specific to repent of? Something so hidden inside of myself that I can no longer remember it? Is it something that hides forgotten on a shelf in the back of my mind? If so, tell me what it is, God, and I will search for it, and repent of it.

And I heard a voice from deep inside my soul say to me, "Do what you need to do, Sarah! Do it now! You know what you have to do! I have told you, but you have not listened to My voice. Listen carefully, Sarah! And whatever you do, don't give up! I am with you. I will help you. The children need you!"

In June, Al and I visited with Grayson again. Grayson did not have much news. He said that no one seems to know anything about the woman named Jeze. Where did she come from? What is her plan? What drives her? How is it that she has such a strong hold over so many people? Can she sustain her control? What is her ultimate goal?

Grayson told us that he had a dream about Jeze. In that dream he confronted her about her behavior. She became furious with him! Grayson said that as a result of his confrontation with her (in the dream), Jeze and her followers all entrenched themselves even further.

Was Grayson's dream just a dream or was it a warning of some kind? If a warning, from whom? Grayson interpreted the dream as a word of "caution," and told us he believes we need to proceed slowly and carefully. But I ask, just how much more slowly can we proceed? We have accomplished nothing . . .

On June 7, 1996, I went out to lunch with some friends and when I returned home I got quite a shock! I had received something in the mail from Annie! It was a manila envelope, and the envelope was thick. Perhaps Annie had written me a long letter of apology? I ripped open the envelope with great expectation, but what I found inside was not good.

I found a letter 13 pages long, notarized and certified. It certainly was not the letter I had been hoping for. It was handwritten and full of hate, accusations, and untruths. She was obviously outraged when she wrote it—mostly at me. All I could think of as I waded through the letter was that this letter could not have possibly come from my daughter! Who was the stranger that had written this? For even though the letter was written in Annie's handwriting, the style and the vocabulary were very different from anything Annie had ever written or spoken before. It was so vicious! Had someone else made her write it? The saddest and most hurtful, most terrible thing of all, was that she began the letter with "Dear Sarah," and not "Dear Mother." Had she totally expunged her mother from her life? Had she totally expunged all of us from her life? I immediately wanted to leave this new world we had built. So I unfolded my wings and soared. And I flew to the beautiful garden to clear my mind and to rest.

The day after I received the letter from Annie,

I went to visit Liz at her home. She looked very old and very tired. I wondered if I looked like that too. Liz could barely focus her thoughts as we were conversing. I told her about Annie's letter and that next week, Al and I were going to see Grayson again. A few others had also agreed to meet with Grayson. Liz said she would go with us.

As we spoke together at her dining room table, one of Liz's daughters, Lila, came into the room and I took the opportunity to ask her if she might have something to share with me concerning my Annie. Lila became very agitated and related that when Annie and Bret lived in the little wing of the house, she was instructed by Annie and Bret that she was never to touch the baby.

Lila also told me that no one in the family was allowed to touch the baby except for Liz. Then Liz added that the baby could never be in the main part of the house with his extended family unless either Annie or Bret was present. And I couldn't help but wonder what Annie and Bret were so afraid of. Were we such frightening people? Did Annie and Bret have to protect little Rory from all of us?

I yearn for tomorrow. My heart is heavy with grief and with sorrow. Tears are lumped in my throat, lodged behind my eyes, and lodged inside my lungs. Who will help me? Who will help the children? Who will save us all? Who? I yearn for tomorrow. For better days. For days of light and color. For days with upturned mouths. For days filled with souls healthy and whole, all back in their places. I yearn for tomorrow. Will not tomorrow come?

On June 20, 1996, Al and I, daughter Kate, Liz, David, and a woman named Connie, all met with Grayson to further our discussion about our children and grandchildren caught up into That Group.

We began by hashing out information we already knew. We wanted to do this first in order to review what we knew and then use that information as a base to add further information. As it turned out, most of the new information that came out of our discussion was about the woman named Jeze. We began to get a picture of who she truly was.

David explained that after Jeze fired all of the church staff (and before she left the church building for a new place), she campaigned heavily to bring Bret and Ray into her inner circle. David spoke about Jeze getting more and more enmeshed in Bret and Ray's lives. David also shared that Jeze "cleansed the brothers of demons and then set them up as elders."

At one time, Jeze's daughter, Theresa, had told her youth group that her mother had been asked to leave a former church because her mother had been practicing witchcraft. Later on, however, after Theresa had been elevated to an elder and was engaged to

Ray, Theresa recanted her story about her mother. Jeze began teaching her followers that anyone outside of *her* church was bound for hell. She also taught that anyone who *left her* church was bound for hell. Therefore, Jeze insisted that all members of *her* church cut off any and all ties with anyone outside of *her* church.

According to David, before Jeze split the church, she would often stand in the back of the sanctuary during the worship services and "stir things up" by chanting loudly or making some other kinds of strange noises. She would also spend time looking for, and finding, demons in members of the congregation. After she discovered the demons, she would follow up by having exorcisms to rid the people of their evil spirits. If these demon-possessed people did not want to submit to Jeze's ranting and raving, they were asked to leave the church.

Unfortunately for her, Jeze rid the church of so many people, by the time she took her group of followers with her to a new location, there were not many people left to follow her.

Another interesting thing about Jeze, according to David, was that she claimed she had the ability to do "astral projection." David also said that she claimed she could both receive and send out messages to her followers using mind vibrations. Jeze also claimed that she had the ability to read people's unopened mail. Basically she claimed that she was in control of all of her followers and if any of them had an impure thought of any kind, she would know about it! David explained that Jeze was very good at instilling *fear* in her followers.

Finally, Connie related a story about a young woman who visited the congregation one Sunday, became frightened over an incident between herself and Jeze, and bolted out the door! She never returned.

After all of us had told Grayson all we could recollect from our experiences, directly or indirectly, with Jeze, we decided to call it a night. We had had enough! The information filled our heads and whirled and whirled around. We did not know what to do next. Grayson told us that he was taking all of the information very seriously. He told us that we needed to be strong. Then he closed the meeting with prayer. I wondered if God would hear Grayson's prayer . . . I wondered where God was.

In late July, Al, Liz, and I met with Grayson again. We talked about possible legal avenues that could be used to get our children out of That Group. We also talked about the fact that there might not be any legal avenues available. I shared Annie's letter with Grayson and the others. Grayson told me that the letter might be used in a court of law as a bit of legal proof that there was something terribly wrong with Annie's mental state. He told us the letter showed that Annie was "out of touch with reality," "extremely angry," and "off the chart" on the MMPI Personality Assessment Scale. Grayson explained that perhaps a lawyer, after examining the letter, would ask the court for a mental competency investigation. In the end, however, we all decided that showing the letter to a lawyer would be too risky and perhaps ruin our relationship with our children and grandchildren forever.

Truth is, at present time, all these years later, we still have not seen any of them since we talked about that letter years ago. Maybe back then we should have gone ahead and tried to do something legally with the letter. Maybe we should have shown someone the letter—someone who knew what to do with it. But we were afraid at the time. Fear was swallowing us up . . .

At present time, I feel alone. From time to time, I have tried to tell others about my daughter's disappearance, but the story is too long and too complicated. I certainly can't tell anyone about the Dark Ones. No one would believe me if I told them. Some listeners have been sympathetic, but very few really want to hear. Perhaps they fear it could happen to their sons and daughters.

> *Now I lay them down to sleep*
> *I pray Thee Lord their souls to keep*
> *And if they die before they wake*
> *I pray Thee Lord their souls to take.*

Chapter 4

IN LATE SUMMER OF 1996, I had a dream that was exceptionally vivid and intense. I dreamed it was night and very dark all around. Al and I were both outside, standing on an unfamiliar street. We were lost. I looked around but could not determine where we were. It was too dark. There were no streetlights. There was no moon. There did not appear to be houses or buildings close by. Where were we? I felt anxious and afraid. I could feel the hair on my arms begin to lift up. Something or someone was coming. We clung together silently, listening for whatever was about to appear. Why were we here? Suddenly we heard footsteps—running footsteps. Who was coming? I closed my eyes and prayed. When I opened them I saw who was coming—just a few yards away now.

It was Annie and Bret. They appeared to be very frightened. Who, or what, were they running from? Suddenly they were upon us, hugging us, and asking us for forgiveness. They were both sobbing hysterically. Then an old battered car appeared out of nowhere, and we all got inside. We knew we were in danger and had to get away. It was then I noticed that both Annie and Bret were covered with dirt. Where in the world had they been? Annie's hair was plastered with mud, and her eyes were too bright.

We drove off in the car with Bret at the wheel. He drove like a maniac. We knew we were fleeing from something evil. Something or someone out there wanted to run us off the road! We peered through the dirty car windows, looking for the Enemy—or Enemies. We felt evil all around. We all feared for our lives! The Dark Ones were coming after us . . . My dark dreams were multiplying. And they were terrifying. I dreamed of Dark Creatures chasing after me. I dreamed of gnarled, menacing tree branches waving at me, trying to grab me. I dreamed of a large, empty building, whispering to me, beckoning me to enter inside its walls. I dreamed of exploding lights wherever I walked. I dreamed of a huge globe of the world, covered with sharp spikes. I dreamed of my daughter crying out to me, and of small children weeping on their pillows, waiting for someone to come rescue them. And I dreamed that no one would come for them. No one . . .

And it came to me that I seemed to exist in three different worlds. I lived in the relatively new world my husband and I had built where my family could live and work and go to school and breathe like ordinary people. I lived in a world of visions where I found myself to be a sparrow among soul-eating owls. And I lived in a dark dream world where dark beings hissed and growled, accused, and destroyed. Surely I was becoming unhinged! And I looked and looked and I could not find God in any of these worlds.

And in the new world my husband and I had built, I continued to tell the people in the congregation that God was near; but I wasn't as sure as I used to be. And I continued to tell the people in the congregation that God always rescues those who call for His help; but I doubted that was always true. Mostly I began agonizing over the partial loss of my faith. Where was God?

Sometime after we received that letter from Annie, Al and I decided to call a lawyer. We had debated with Grayson and the others about whether we needed to try to do anything legally about getting our grown children and grandchildren out of That Group they belonged to. We had discussed Annie's letter. Then we had decided as a group that we would not do anything at all. Too risky!

However, Al and I were having second thoughts about Annie's letter. It was just so strange! Maybe we needed someone else to look at that letter, to get a second opinion of what, if anything, could be done. So Al called a lawyer about our situation, and we told him about our daughter and That Group she belonged to. Amazingly, he listened to us and seemed concerned.

I was surprised at his response because I did not expect him to believe us. But he believed us and told us he could assign one of the lawyers in his firm to work with us, but that it would be very expensive to proceed and there would be no guarantees of a positive outcome. Then he told us it was almost impossible to extricate family members from cult-like groups. Annie and Bret were adults, and we couldn't just go in and kidnap them. He said that we could try to extricate our grandson. But we would have to have Annie and Bret declared as unfit parents. Bottom line: we could try to get Rory out, but it would cost many dollars. And the chances of getting Rory out would be low. We thanked him and said we needed some time to think about everything. Then we asked ourselves: Did we have enough resources to pay for all the costs involved? Would we risk further wrath from our daughter and her family if we moved on this? Would moving forward be worth the risk? We didn't know. Would the outcome be in our favor? We didn't know.

In the end, we decided not to go forward. We decided that we needed to wait and pray. Either way we were taking a risk. Maybe things would work out . . . maybe they would not. Today, looking back, I don't know if we made the right decision. We will never know for sure.

One thing I was sure of—Al and I were tired of all of the hurt and pain that continued to seep into the new world we had created. We needed to try to wipe out the pain and get on with our lives! We needed to get on with work, school, the family we had, and our friends, etc. But how? How could we move on in the midst of hurting so much! What we needed to do and what we were able to do were two very different things!

> *Hear my voice, O Lord, when I call; have mercy on me and answer me. My heart speaks your message, 'Seek my face.' Your face, O Lord, will I seek. Hide not your face from me, turn not away. You have been my helper; forsake me not, O God of my salvation (Psalm 27:7-9).*

On August 23, 1996, Al and I went to see Grayson again. During our time together, Grayson told us that he believed Ray was a key figure to That Group, and that if Ray fell, they would all fall—like dominoes. He said we all needed to pray continually for Ray's deliverance!

But after our meeting with Grayson I asked myself, "How could an alcoholic and former drug addict (Ray) possibly have any power or influence over anyone?" Yet, Ray was apparently Jeze's 'Chosen One.' He was married to Jeze's daughter, and they already had several children. Not only that, according to former members who had witnessed Ray and Jeze together, Ray and Jeze seemed to be inseparable—even though there was a 30-year age difference between them! How strange! How inappropriate! They certainly lived in a world vastly different from the world I used to live in—in the world where I was ordinarily Sarah, living an ordinary life in an ordinary world!

In October, I had yet another dream about Annie. I dreamed that a big man—a dark and menacing man— was persecuting Al and I and our two other daughters. He was telling us what to think, how to live, and what to believe. He kept hounding and hounding! Annie appeared and she kept encouraging the big man, and kept encouraging the rest of us to believe the big man. Her eyes were gleaming, just like the big man's eyes were gleaming.

Why were their eyes gleaming? Why were their mouths so twisted? Why did their voices sound so strange? Where was my real daughter? This daughter could not be the daughter I knew and loved. Suddenly another man burst into the scene. He had a gun and began shooting. He shot the big man right in the middle of his chest, dead. We ran away—fast—all except for Annie. She stayed behind. Why didn't she run with us? What is to become of her?

In early November I had two more nightmares on two consecutive nights. In the first one, a Dark Creature was stalking me. I was walking outside, trying to find my way home, but I couldn't find my way because it was dark all around. There were no streetlights: no porch lights from the houses I knew were lined up and down the street, there was no moon, and there were no stars. The Dark Creature was getting closer! I could feel his breath on the back of my neck. Then the creature began to threaten me. He said he wanted to kill me. If I could only find the light . . . In the second dream, I was outside again, and again it was dark. I found myself in a forest. This time I was unable to move. My feet would not move. A huge, gnarled tree bent its branches low to the ground and began waving them at me, menacingly. Then the entire tree began moving towards me and I could do nothing but stand there and watch. Closer and closer it came and began to entangle me in its skinny, barren branches. I thought to myself, "I am going to die."Then I had yet another nightmare! They just kept coming! This time the evil entity was an old church building— a large cathedral—made of stone that was cold, unfriendly, and uncomfortable looking. The caretakers, a man and a woman, lived and worked in the building. They also were cold, unfriendly, and uncomfortable looking—larger than life and somewhat misshapen. They had small dark eyes and thin unsmiling lips. They beckoned to me, wanting me to go inside, but I declined and ran away—fast.

I don't know what all of these dreams mean. Maybe they don't mean anything at all. If they do mean something, that something is a riddle. I felt evil in all of the dreams. Evil all around me, trying to bring me down. But I don't want to think of evil things. I don't want to think of Dark Creatures or gnarled trees or dark unfriendly buildings. I want to make it all go away—to get the bad dreams out of my mind. I don't want to be frightened! But I am frightened!

Hear me, O God! I'm not brave. I'm not strong. I don't know how to fight Evil. I don't know how to fight Dark Creatures. Help me please, God! Please come and help me!

In late November, Al and I met with Dan and Liz at a local restaurant near their home. Liz was a bit agitated. She told us that she had driven over to Ray's apartment in hopes she might catch a glimpse of him. Apparently she drives over there from time to time, and on occasion does see him in the parking lot. (How horrible for her that she has to sneak around to see her son!) Liz told us that she saw him this last time she had gone over there. He was in his car with his wife, Theresa, right outside their apartment. Liz had stopped her car, gotten out, and walked over to their stopped car, hoping to speak with them. Ray and Theresa would not roll down their car windows to speak with her as she approached them. They made no attempt to make eye contact with her, either. Then, after a few awkward moments, with Liz standing on the driver's side of the car, Theresa began yelling at Liz through the rolled up windows, "Go away! You have forfeited all of your rights!" Not a pretty picture. Maybe Liz would have been better off to just leave them alone. Ray and Theresa won't change their attitude toward her. They are "dug in," just like Bret and Annie.

After the four of us finished our lunch, we decided

to drive to a local strip mall. Someone had told Liz that the group our grown children belonged to was renting a space in the mall for their meetings. (They had moved from a hotel lobby to a strip mall.) We were not sure if we wanted to see their space or not, but it was the middle of the day and their space was located in a public area, so we decided to go.

We climbed in our car and in minutes arrived at our destination. Then, after parking our car, we cautiously got out, walked up to the entranceway, and slipped through the front doors to the strip mall. The mall was small, so we didn't have to look far. Suddenly, there it was—a space with a sign on the door that named their group. We looked in the window and could see the piano inside (the very one that Al and I had given to Annie and Bret).

We also saw a very large and very strange poster hanging on the interior wall of their space. The poster was more than strange; it was creepy. It looked like a picture of the world with ugly spikes sticking out all over it (sort of like the dream I'd had of Annie's womb with spikes sticking out all over it). An information sheet was adhered to the front door with the pastors' names listed. But no phone numbers were listed nor were there any hours listed for times of worship. *Strange.* The skin on the back of my neck prickled as I took it all in. Then I began to walk away, and the others followed. We all felt shaken . . . this was no dream!

As the weeks and months went by something very

strange began happening to me. All kinds of glass things began exploding in my presence—lamp bulbs, refrigerator bulbs as I swung open refrigerator doors, glass figurines in fancy cases, small lights lining sidewalk paths as I walked by them. Everywhere I went, glass was exploding! What was going on! This was no dream! This was really happening!

In late November I had another nightmare. I dreamed I was a prisoner in a jail somewhere and in danger. I had my cell phone with me and I tried to call someone for help. I could not reach anyone—no one at all! I was terrified! I believed I was going to die! The Dark Creatures had locked me up and were going to kill me! Soon! I was sure of it! I was having so many nightmares. What did they mean? Was I losing my grip? Had I gone insane?

DECEMBER 10, 1996

I had yet another frightening nightmare. Scores of evil creatures were chasing after me. I needed to escape. And fast! I became the little brown sparrow, unfolded my wings, and flew away to the beautiful garden, hoping God would meet me there.

Liz called me a bit further into December. She found out that a man by the name of Evin and his wife Bella, both previously active members of That Group, had left the group! Apparently some of the elders had been trying to convince Evin to divorce Bella and marry someone else. Bella had become despondent over this and had tried to kill herself. Evin walked in on Bella before she could complete the act and he put a stop to it.

Then, apparently, they both "woke up" and left That Group. Soon after their departure, Evin called a church in Georgia where Jeze had been a member at one time. He spoke with the senior pastor of that church, and that pastor warned Evin to keep away from Jeze.

Grayson also called me in December with some interesting news. He had moved to a new, more spacious office located in the little strip mall where That Group met. I hadn't spoken to him in a number of months, so he hadn't been told That Group had also relocated there. Grayson explained to me that his new office is huge and that he now has enough space to expand his counseling ministry! His plans include starting up a foundation to help "wounded Christians"—especially those who have been attacked by entities from the "Dark Side." He further shared that he had plans to offer worship services in his new space, as well as Bible studies, and live, inspirational presentations given by guest teachers and preachers!

And then came the real shocker! By some bizarre twist of fate, Grayson's new office is located in the space right next to That Group's space in that little strip mall! Grayson was totally amazed when he discovered that! He believes that God has most certainly had a hand in the situation!

Chapter 5

DECEMBER 21, 1996

I have been sitting in the small cafeteria at a Walmart for the last 15 minutes, waiting for Liz to finish her shift. Suddenly I feel the hairs on the back of my neck lift up and I look around, afraid that one of the Dark Angels is nearby. But I do not see anything unusual, and, in fact, everything looks quite normal—people are rushing about doing their last minute Christmas shopping, a Salvation Army worker is ringing his bell and accepting donations into his kettle, the sounds of Christmas songs are soaring throughout the store, and all things sparkle. I wonder if my daughter misses me. I wonder if she will think of me on Christmas morning. But it is easier if I just don't think about it. If I just don't think about her.

Liz finally arrived. It was good to see her, although seeing her instantly brought up the problem of our children. I wanted to be with Liz, and I didn't want to be with her at all. For a moment, I became anxious and I looked around expecting to see a Dark Creature slinking behind the food counter or hiding behind a shopper. But there were no Dark Creatures; we were safe for now. We talked for a while and then we reluctantly decided that we should go over to our children's apartments and bring our grandchildren their Christmas presents. We also talked about actually trying to see them, but then decided it would be better if we just left the gifts outside of their apartment doors, rang their doorbells, and then ran for it. How bizarre that it had come to this. Two loving grandmothers, merely wanting to see their grandchildren and bring them Christmas gifts, and all they can do is leave the gifts by the doors, ring the doorbells, and run.

But that expedition would have to wait for a little while. Liz had a great deal of things to tell me. She told me she had decided to attend a worship service at the church where Annie and Bret had gotten married. A friend had told her that the church was functioning again and many of its former members had returned. Liz went, and there she saw David, Evin, Bella, and the former pastor, as well as others. She told me that everyone was kind and welcoming to her. And Evin spoke to her for quite a while. Evin told her that they were all praying for our children and grandchildren. He told her that his wife, Bella, had groups of people at her place of work praying for our kids and grandkids also. Evin also told Liz that he had driven all the way to Georgia, to Jeze's former church, so he could sit down face-to-face with her former pastor. Evin said he spoke with that pastor for about eight hours.

The pastor told Evin that Jeze had gone through some kind of "deliverance ceremony" while she was in Georgia, and afterwards she began twisting truths, became controlling, and began to exhibit "supernatural powers." The leaders of her Georgia church asked her to leave sometime after, as she had become a "Deceiver" and a "Dangerous Woman." Jeze then left Georgia, moved here, and found a new church home.

Liz also found out that Jeze's husband, Jeb, was upset that Ray and Bret and their wives had not been allowed to attend Maria's funeral. Apparently Jeze has full control of her husband.

Liz also learned something from a young woman named Tina, who was told she had to leave That Group because of a small infraction she had committed. Before she left, Tina was made to stand in front of Ray, who had been elevated to the position of Senior Pastor, and she had to look him in the eye for a long period of time while he glared at her.

Then the remaining members of That Group encircled them and taunted her while Ray screamed at her. Tina told Liz that when Ray finally let her go, she was glad she had gotten away alive!

And I wonder why these former members of That Group don't go to the authorities! Something seems terribly wrong inside That Group—and something seems terribly wrong with the people who have seen That Group from the inside, have left it, and then have done nothing to help the others they left behind. What were they afraid of?

And I wondered if perhaps Liz and I should go to the authorities (the police) ourselves? But would they listen to secondhand information? The only thing we had to show the police was Annie's bizarre letter to me—nothing else, except what we could tell them about the strange things we have experienced ourselves. But we had no *real* proof of anything abusive or illegal.

Were we merely blowing the whole situation out of proportion? Were we simply two quirky ladies with over-active imaginations? Would anyone take us seriously? Or would they simply see us as two hysterical mothers/grandmothers spouting out strange stories about a woman with supernatural powers who kidnapped our children and grandchildren? Who would listen to that? Maybe that is why the others won't talk. Maybe they don't think anyone will believe them either. Or maybe they are afraid of what Jeze might do if she found out that they were talking to others about That Group.

> *Now I lay them down to sleep.*
> *I pray thee Lord their souls to keep.*
> *And if they die before they wake,*
> *I pray thee Lord their souls to take.*

DECEMBER 28, 1996

Light bulbs keep exploding at a steady rate as I enter each room in my house. They are also exploding as I enter rooms in other people's houses; I can't understand it. But it has happened so many times it doesn't bother me much anymore—except when a glass figurine exploded in my sister's curio cabinet as

I entered her dining room. It exploded right before our eyes! But how? I did not know. But it did. Amazingly, I was beginning to take these strange happenings in stride.

I had another nightmare. A dozen or so hideous demons were after me. I screamed and screamed! Al woke up and shook me so that I would wake up also. I was so relieved to see his face. Those demons were so angry with me! They wanted to kill me! Why are there so many hideous creatures in my world of dreams?

JANUARY, 1997

I had hoped the New Year would be a better year for all of us, but it began with another nightmare for me. It was very vivid and extremely detailed. Annie, Bret, and little Rory were all in it. The dream began with explosions, earthquakes, trees falling down, buildings falling down, people running everywhere— all trying to find a safe place. I was running, too. Where to go? I was terrified!

As the dream continued, I somehow ended up

in Annie and Bret's apartment. It was quiet there, and nothing out of the ordinary was going on. I was surprised they let me come in. At first Annie was timid, as if she did not know what to say to me, then she held out her arms for a hug. Bret was in the back room and did not come out to greet me, but he did not seem to object to my being there. Little Rory was at the kitchen table eating. He did not know who I was, but did not object to my presence. I was able to talk to him for a while. Annie began telling me about her "church." She said the church could not pay its bills and that people were leaving. Then I woke up. The dream was over. I felt sad. I missed my daughter so much—and my little grandson. And Bret.

> *O Jesus, grant me hope and comfort;*
> *O let me ne're in sorrow pine,*
> *My heart and soul, yea, all my being,*
> *O Jesus trust alone in thee.*
> *Thou Prince of Peace, Thou Pearl from*
> *heaven,*
> *True God, true Man, my Morning Star!*
> *—From O Jesus, Grant Me Hope and*
> *Comfort*
> *By Johann Wolfgang Franck*

Liz and I still have had no response from the kids regarding the gifts we left for them just before Christmas. Nothing at all. We should not have wasted our money. They most likely threw everything out or gave it all away. But maybe not. I just don't know what to think about anything anymore. I wonder if Annie thinks of me as she begins the New Year. Does she think of any of us who she left behind? If so, how? With fear? Anger? Disgust? Sorrow? If only she could come back to us.

JANUARY 5, 1997

I had another vivid dream. I was in the kids' apartment again. Annie and Bret both greeted me, and Annie brought little Rory out to see me. He was so much bigger than when I last saw him! There was another child present—a girl. It was a lovely dream.

JANUARY 9, 1997

Liz called me during the evening with some new information. Tom, a young man and divorced father of two small children and member of That Group, had just cut off all ties with his parents. Tom's parents are Jason and Carrie, and Jason is a practicing attorney. Jason has begun the process of getting visitation rights with their grandchildren, Paulie and Cassie. This might be good news for the rest of us! I will call Jason's office in the morning. Perhaps he might be able to help Liz and me and our families!

JANUARY 10, 1997

This day I found myself speaking with Jason. Jason and Carrie were to have a court hearing in a few weeks. They were suing for grandparent visitation rights. We spoke for quite a while. He told me he would get in touch with me after the hearing.

JANUARY 20, 1997

Jason called our home, and Al spoke with him at length. Jason said that he had met with his lawyer, Marilyn, and she felt that they had a good case. A petition was filed. Interestingly, two sets of grandparents have now filed for grandparent visitation rights. Carrie and Jason (Tom's parents and grandparents to Tom's children) and Bill and Betty (parents of Tom's ex-wife and also grandparents to Tom's children). Apparently the children's mother is not in the picture at all. Jeze ran the children's mother out of the church. We don't know if she is still married to Tom or not, but do know that there was a lot of pressure put on Tom to divorce her. Apparently, Jeze's group painted a very dark picture of her for Tom and told him he needed to leave her.

The Dark Ones named Intimidation, Force, Hatred, and Manipulation were in full force the day Jeze told Tom to leave his wife!

Grayson called. He has seen several of That Group's members outside of their meeting place. Grayson said that they meet on Wednesday and Friday evenings. One of the members, a big hulky guy, stands guard at the entrance of their meeting place and monitors all who go in and out. It appears as if only the present members of That Group are allowed in. Then, when everyone is inside, all of the shades are closed, the front door is locked, and the lights go out (at least from what Grayson can see from the hallway outside of their space).

They don't appear to be a welcoming organization! But what do I know about anything in this strange new world I am living in!

> *Hey diddle diddle,*
> *The cat and the fiddle,*
> *The cow jumped over the moon.*
> *The little dog laughed to see such a*
> *sport,*
> *And the dish ran away with the spoon!*
> *—A children's nursery rhyme*

JANUARY 29, 1997

Al and I met with Dan and Liz and Jason and Carrie. Jason and Carrie told us they had been doing lots of babysitting for Tom's two children before he was ordered to cut off ties to his family. This fact could help them in trying to get grandparent rights to the children.

They also related some disturbing facts about Paulie and Cassie (Tom's children). Apparently Paulie (4) and Cassie (2) have been exhibiting some bizarre behavior. Paulie keeps telling his grandparents that Cassie is "full of demons." (What four-year-old knows about demons?) They also explained that from time to time Paulie describes himself as a "bad boy" and then punishes himself! He will not watch TV or play with his toys as a form of punishment for himself. (Again, what four-year-old would say and do those things?)

Liz and Dan also had some strange things to add to our conversation. Apparently Evin had related to Liz that he had seen a bruise on Rory's face. Not only that, it was Bret who had put it there! Also, according to Evin, Paulie and Cassie were regularly spanked by the males in the group—full force (meaning open hands) because "They were full of demons!" It is all so disturbing! Why doesn't Evin go to the proper authorities? He has seen the abuse first hand. What is he waiting for? What is he afraid of? How can he sleep at night? Have the Dark Ones in his life grown so powerful that he can no longer make good decisions?

Liz called me later with some startling news. She told me that Carrie had called DCFS and "turned them all in." It is about time that someone with firsthand information called Children's Services!

Liz also related that Evin is now confessing to her that abuse *is* definitely going on inside That Group— towards the children, as well as the adults. If only he, too, would contact Children's Services, or perhaps the police department!

EARLY FEBRUARY 1997

I called the DCFS hotline to report the bruise on Rory's cheek. Unfortunately, all I had was second- and thirdhand information to relate. I sensed that the woman at the other end of the phone was not taking me seriously. She told me to call the local office. I felt like I was totally dismissed. Maybe I could get some of the others with firsthand information to call?

Many calls are going back and forth from me to Liz, to Grayson, and to Carrie, and to others who are concerned about the children in That Group. We are all going to get together for a meeting at Liz and Dan's house. Maybe, with all of us together in one place, we can figure out where to go from there regarding the children's safety. We made a list of people to invite. Many of those on the list are former members of either the original little church where Annie and Bret got married or are former members of That Group—or both. All of these people have had dealings with Jeze and many have seen, first hand, the abuse of both children and adults under her leadership.

As it turned out, not everyone on our list was able to attend the meeting, but the few who did show up were able to relay some information to the rest of us.

Some of that information included the following:

During That Group's "worship services," parents are asked if any of their children have been "bad" during the week prior to the service. If it is determined that some of the children have misbehaved at home in any way, they are punished—most usually by having them stand against the wall for 2 or 3 hours at a time or until the "service" ends, which often goes on for 3 hours or more.

Ray (Senior Pastor) rants and raves during his "sermons" and is the voice that "pronounces harsh judgments" on children and adults when they misbehave.

One former member explained that there are two separate "groups" of people who attend the "services." One group, the "condemned group," must sit on the left side of the room. The other group, the "righteous group," has the honor of sitting on the right side of the room. (Family members often had to sit on different sides of the room, depending on who was condemned and/or who was righteous for that particular week.) Usually, the group's leaders and their families sat on the right and everyone else sat on the left.

The people on the left are not allowed to speak to the people on the right. Therefore, some husbands are not able to speak to their wives and vice versa, and some parents are not able to speak to their children and vice versa. The "silence" between family members might last for a week or more, or for however long it takes for the condemned to get in good graces with their leaders (the righteous ones). Apparently, during the "services," Ray, the main preacher and voice piece for Jeze, spends a lot of time screaming at and berating the people in the "condemned" group.

A former member said she was asked by Jeze to divorce her husband, as he was not a member of That Group. This former member also said that at times, she was afraid for her life, as well as the lives of her husband and daughter. She went on to say that Ray abused her and her daughter, as well as other children and adults.

What will it take, Lord, for You to come
to the rescue of Your people?
With what shall I come before the Lord
and bow
down before the exalted God?
Shall I come before him with burnt
offerings, with
calves a year old?
Will the Lord be pleased with thousands
of rams, with
ten thousand rivers of olive oil?
Shall I offer my first born for my
transgression,
The fruit of my body for the sin of my
soul?

—Micah 6:6-7

FEBRUARY 1, 1997

Carrie told me that she did not think DCFS was taking her seriously; I was not surprised. What is it with this organization? Don't they exist to help children? But then again, they all live in "That Other World"—the world I first lived in. Perhaps they don't understand about Dark Angels. Perhaps they don't believe that other worlds do exist.

FEBRUARY 2, 1997

The day after I spoke with Carrie, I called DCFS myself—at the local field office. I spoke with a Ms. Wendell. I tried to explain to her that my grandchildren were involved with a cultic religious group, and I feared they were being harmed. There was not a lot of response from her at first, so I rattled on and on for quite a while, wondering if she believed anything I was telling her. When I finally finished, she asked me some questions and then told me to call her back the next day!

FEBRUARY 3, 1997

Carrie spoke with a young woman by the name of Suzanne. Suzanne, a young adult, was the daughter of two members of That Group. Suzanne had also been a member of That Group for a time, but eventually left. Then she explained to Carrie that right after she left, her parents disowned her. Suzanne also told Carrie that she left That Group because she believed the children were being degraded. She also believed the atmosphere of That Group was dangerous, and added that Ray had totally lost control of himself and had become cruel and sadistic. Suzanne also reported to Carrie that one of the members of That Group got caught with child pornography in his possession and was punished by the leaders of That Group but was still a member. As far as punishments go, Suzanne explained to Carrie that both children and adults were often punished for their sins days after the sins were committed! Finally, Suzanne said that she had been receiving harassing phone calls from the leaders of That Group ever since she left.

But why did she give Carrie all of this information? Why not the police? What kind of hold do the leaders of this religious group have over their members?

I miss my daughter so much. Where has she gone? Where have all of them gone? I wish I could find some peace. But there is no peace to be found.

FEBRUARY 6, 1997

Three days after speaking to Carrie, I called Ms. Wendell at DCFS again. She told me that she was in the process of trying to interview Annie and Bret but that Bret had been uncooperative and unresponsive to all of the attempts she had made to reach him. I was not surprised. I was certain that he did not want to talk to her. I was very grateful that she was doing this.

What a dark world I live in most of my waking hours. Will light ever come to stay? Will God ever come? My family and I try our best to stay in the new world we have created for ourselves; we keep on working, going to school, and breathing so that we can live. We keep on smiling. And we keep on looking for the light, however dim.

In the beginning was the Word, and the Word was with God, and the Word was God. He was with God in the beginning.

Through him all things were made that has been made. In him was life and that life was the light of all people. The light shines in the darkness, but the darkness has not understood it. . . . He was in the world, and though the world was made through him, the world did not recognize him. He came to that which was his own, but his own did not receive him (John 1:1-11).

FEBRUARY 8, 1997

I spoke to Carrie again. She was so upset! She said she hated Jeze! She said she wanted more information about That Group! She explained that she had sent Valentine's Day cards to her grandkids (Paulie and Cassie) and Tom returned them with a scathing note telling her that she had no respect for him or his family. To top it all off, he addressed her as "Carrie," not as "Mom"! I told her my Annie had also sent me a scathing letter and had it addressed as "Dear Sarah." I also told her about the conversation Al and I had with our state representative. She was interested in what I had to say and suggested that she and her husband join with us in our efforts to get our grandchildren out of That Group; however, she said she needed to speak with her husband first. I didn't know if her husband would want to engage in any legal proceedings other than getting visitation rights to his grandchildren. He is a lawyer himself; he has his reputation and his family's reputation to protect.

I hope I am wrong. But I believe he will do what

he has to do in a very quiet way with a lawyer that he knows will keep the process discreet. Besides, Al and I had thought it would be better if we did not go forward with any litigation at this point in time.

The Dark One named Fear rules! It rules all of us. And I am terrified! But I don't want anyone to know I am terrified!

"Terrified" is easy to hide. A big smile and a confident air and an upper thrust of the chin takes care of "Terrified." "Sadness" is harder to bury, but somehow I have managed to hide it. From the very beginning, I have not cried much over Annie. Crying would make the nightmare real, and I did not want it to be real. But inside of me, where no one can see, I have stuffed away millions of tears. And they wait for the moment when I will finally give in to them. But they wait in vain. I will not give in to them! If I give in to them, I might never stop. There are too many of them. It would take the rest of my life to rid myself of them! And so I stuff them all into a tear box. I wish now I would have let myself cry in the beginning of it all. I could have emptied myself of much hurt and anger, of much of the sadness. Instead, I decided to be brave and not show any emotion at all. I have so much hidden inside of me that no one sees—that no one knows about.

The "me" I show in my newly-constructed world is shallow and stunted. This "me" looks okay on the surface. It would appear as if I have it all together: I smile. I go to work. I enjoy my family and friends. And no one knows that I live in other worlds.

My God! My God! Why have You forsaken me? Have I done something so terrible that You won't show Your face to me?

FEBRUARY 8, 1997, LATER IN THE DAY

Liz called and told me she had received a letter from Evin. He wrote that he and his wife wanted to forget about That Group. They wanted to forget all that had happened to them inside the group. Evin explained that they had been deeply hurt by false accusations from the group's leaders, and that they had received threatening letters from these people. At this point, they just wanted to move on with their lives and were unable to help us. They told Liz they were sorry, and they promised to pray for us.

On the one hand, I don't blame this couple for wanting to move on. It is all so frightening. But on the other hand, there are innocent children involved. How can they move on and leave the children behind?

This group has hurt so many people, and the ripples of that hurt continue to move outward. When is it going to end? How many people will the leaders of this group destroy along the way?

I beg You, God, show Your face!

Chapter 6

FEBRUARY 9, 1997

Grayson called. He said he was in the process of having his office remodeled, and that his firewall had been temporarily removed. He was in his office last evening when That Group was having their "worship service," and he heard everything the group was doing through his paper-thin wall. He told me that things really "got out of hand" as the worship service dragged on. He said he believes That Group and its leaders are very dangerous at this point in time.

He told me the worship service went from 7:00pm to 10:30pm and that there was a lot of yelling, shouting, condemning, and judgment-calling going on. In fact, it was almost constant. Worried, he decided to go into the public hallway outside of the offices. He did, and he looked at the outside of the space where That Group worshipped. He found that all the blinds on the windows were closed and that there were no lights on inside their gathering place. All of the shouting, etc., was going on in the dark! And he heard children crying throughout the entire ordeal!

Then at one point during the "service," Grayson said he began to hear strange incantations. He did not recognize the words at first. They were not in English or any other language he had ever heard. Finally he began to hear, in English, prayers for the deaths of Al and Sarah. Over and over he heard them praying for our deaths! That was when Grayson decided he needed to go to the police!

As a result of that conversation with Grayson, Al got on the phone and began calling various people in our county—including our state representative, the county sheriff, the state's attorney, and others— basically anyone in public office who we thought might be able to help us.

Were the Dark Ones inside of That Group intent on actually killing us? Who would help us? Anyone? Anyone at all? And when? Must we be murdered in our beds before anyone intervenes?

Dear God, show Your face!

FEBRUARY 10, 1997

I called DCFS. They were out of the office until Tuesday due to a holiday. Then we called the police department and spoke with a detective, and we made an appointment to go see him. We decided we would tell him everything we knew—names, phone numbers, addresses, everything! Grayson called again and told us he had been to the police. He said he had told them everything that he had heard during that worship service. Grayson believed that he and his co-workers would be in grave danger if the members of That Group found out he had "ratted" on them!

Grayson also told us he was very frightened for us. He said the police explained to him that all of us just needed to stay back and let them do their work. It appeared as if somebody was going to do something to help us after all!

FEBRUARY 13, 1997

I am having fears that murderers are going to burst into our home and gun us all down!

February moved along. We decided to have another meeting at Liz and Dan's house, and we did. Those present included: Jason and Carrie, Al and myself, Dan and Liz, Bill and Betty, Kate, Connie, Dori, Grayson, and Tessa. Along with these people, Evin and Bella sent a letter for us to read. These people were all either extended family members of people involved in That Group or were former members. All of them were hurting. We all knew we needed to do something to get our children and grandchildren out of That Group. We just didn't know what! A number of things were spoken of during that meeting:

> Carrie volunteered that she had spoken
> with the police. Two detectives have been
> assigned to our case—Detective Charles
> and Detective Banion (a juvenile officer).

Bill and Betty (Tom's in-laws) related that at one point in time, Paulie (their grandson) was not allowed to visit them because he had been "a bad boy," and therefore had to stay with Ray for a few days so that Ray could change Paulie into "a good boy."

Dori, (former member of That Group) related that letters (from Jeze) were sent to her two teenage daughters while they were all still a part of the church where Annie and Bret were married. The letters were scathing and abusive.

Dori confirmed that Jeze prophesied 5 marriages and a number of divorces at their former church.

Dori explained that at one point, she had to go before Evin and Bella, as well as Jeze and a handful of others, for "judgment." They were verbally abusive to her and told her that she was a witch.

Dori also related that the children were regularly spanked during worship—even very young children. It was a way of punishing them for their sins.

Finally, Dori said that she had decided to leave That Group because she was frightened the church leaders would hurt her or her family.

Tessa (also a former member of That Group) explained about an incident in which she was late to a meeting. When she finally arrived at the meeting, all of the group members made a circle around her and began taunting her. Then Ray began making strange noises, put a thin veil over his face, and said to her in a menacing way, "Look at me. You are to leave the church and never come back! Have you no shame? Cover your eyes when you look toward my face!"

Tessa also explained what all of us already knew: group members were told they must cut off ties with former family members and former friends. They needed to cut off all ties to their pasts! Tessa was told that former family and friends would defile their children if ties were not cut.

Evin, (former Group member) related, via his letter, that he had seen little Paulie and other children stand in corners for lengthy periods of time during worship services as punishment for various sins. He stated that once he saw little Paulie standing in a corner for 3-4 hours. He also wrote that he did not want to get involved with the police or any other type of authority, as he believed doing so would put him and his entire family in harm's way.

Grayson (Christian counselor for those hurt by That Group) shared with us that the police and DCFS were interested in helping the children and were willing to work together. (We were all somewhat encouraged with that news!) Grayson also told us, and the police, that when he heard the worship service going on, he heard children screaming—frightened screaming! He also heard a woman, whom he believed was Jeze, calling on the "Powers" from the North, South, East, and West to bring judgment and death upon Al and Sarah.

This entire situation was even worse than we had thought! But we did not have any hard evidence of anything! And no one with firsthand information was willing to go to the authorities. Everyone was frightened! It was entirely possible that no one in authority would be able to help us!

The Dark Ones that have invaded our lives are cunning, demeaning, and frightening! They have scooped up our souls, turned them into unrecognizable entities, and have—almost entirely—devoured them.

Satan himself masquerades as an angel of light. It is not surprising, then, if his servants masquerade as servants of righteousness (2 Corinthians 11: 14-15a).

And I still did not want to hear it. I still did not want to believe it . . . but I prayed anyway:

Our Father, who art in Heaven,
Hallowed be thy Name,
Thy kingdom come,
Thy will be done,

ORDINARILY SARAH

On earth, as it is in Heaven.
Give us this day our daily bread,
And forgive us our debts,
As we forgive our debtors.
And lead us not into temptation,
But deliver us from evil
For thine is the kingdom, and the power
and the glory
Forever and ever. Amen

PART 2

There is so much darkness in this world, but too often we refuse to see it, refuse to get involved, refuse to risk being uncomfortable.

Forgive us, Lord!

Chapter 7

FEBRUARY 16, 1997

A detective named Lawrence spent three hours with us in our home. He asked all kinds of questions about the group our daughter belonged to and the alleged "death threats" made toward us. He wanted all of the members' names, all of their phone numbers, all of their license plate numbers. We gave him what we could.

The detective advised us to begin keeping a "phone log" and jot down any unusual phone calls or "hang ups." He also advised us to purchase deadbolt locks for our outside doors and to devise an emergency escape plan should we feel threatened by anyone. Further, he told us to report to him any suspicious boxes or packages placed near our house.

He asked us if we owned any firearms. We told him no. Finally, he explained that we needed a peephole in both outside doors and a safe place to hide, if necessary. He also said we each needed to carry a phone at all times. Our time with the detective was unsettling. Was this visit from Detective Lawrence just another nightmare? I asked my husband if Detective Lawrence was real; Al said he was.

And I wished I could go back to my old world, the world where I knew nothing about Dark Angels, the Prince of Darkness, detectives, and suffering children. But then, much of that old world had been make believe. It was a world I had put together with paper and glue, strings and staples. It was a world where all was well and evil did not exist. And that world fell apart on that Terrible Day when the Sky Turned Black.

FEBRUARY 17, 1997

Al and I made the hour-long trip for our first meeting with Detective Charles, the officer Grayson has been working with. We picked up Liz and Carrie at their homes so that we could all arrive at the police department together. I felt terrified going through the double doors of the police station. I had never been to a police station in my life! I felt sick to my stomach, light headed, panicky, and off kilter. Did the others feel the same way? They did not appear to be nervous! In fact, they seemed calm and self-assured. What was wrong with me? Why did I feel like a criminal? Why did I feel like a woman who was about to waste somebody's time? I so wanted to be invisible. But I could not make myself invisible—not as long as all the others were with me! Nor could I unfold my little sparrow wings and fly to the ceiling! I needed to be with all the others. All of me!

Detective Charles appeared to be quite young, perhaps in his early 30s: tall and lean, but not an imposing figure at all. His demeanor? He seemed half interested and mostly bumbling. He didn't say much, just asked lots of questions. When it was my turn to speak, I stumbled and stuttered also. I must have looked like a very foolish woman. And I so wanted him to take us seriously! But I wasn't able to say anything remotely coherent. (At least, that's the way I felt). And when our time was over, my gut told me he most probably did not believe much of anything we told him. Then again, why would he? Our story was preposterous!

He did write down everything we told him, but he did not look concerned. He looked like he was just doing his job. He looked tired and bored. In the end, I left feeling anxious and unsettled. He did give us his card, however, and his cellphone number, saying that we could call him if anything more developed. He then added that he would call DCFS soon. I wondered what he meant by "soon."

FEBRUARY 20, 1997

I had another nightmare last night. A creature was stalking me, and he had a shotgun. Suddenly he opened fire at me. I was prepared to die, but then a man jumped out of the darkness and began firing at the creature and shot him dead. I collapsed in relief.

Would my family miss me if a murderer killed me? Or would they pretend that I never existed and just go on with their lives as usual? Or if they thought

I had existed, would they attend my funeral? Would there even be a funeral for them to attend?

FEBRUARY 21, 1997

I spoke to Ms. Wendell, from the local Department of Family and Children's Services. She told me she had spoken with Annie and Bret. Finally! Ms. Wendell said that their house was immaculate and that little Rory appeared to be affectionate and well cared for. She also told me that Bret was so nervous he broke out in hives as they were speaking. Then she mentioned that Annie was holding a new baby.

I could not even begin to express my surprise at that news! How could Annie not tell us about their new child? I asked Ms. Wendell about the sex of the baby and its name. She would not give me that information. She seemed upset with herself at even mentioning the fact that Annie and Bret had a new baby! (Was this the baby I had dreamed about nine months ago?)

Ms. Wendell did tell me she was working with Detective Charles. We talked for quite a while. Both she and the police would like to see what is going on inside That Group. She asked me lots of questions. At the end of our conversation, I thanked her for her efforts, but my gut told me I would probably not hear from her again. It would be impossible for her, or the police, to get inside That Group. I was sure that no one inside That Group would ever sit down and have a conversation with anyone on the outside; anyone on the outside of their group was thought of as evil.

FEBRUARY 23, 1997

We had a number of people in mind who we thought might help us get some information about Annie and Bret's new baby. And with some work, we finally did get that information from a friend of Liz who worked at the hospital. She told Liz that the baby was born on January 29, 1997. She would not give any more information, but at least we knew the birth date!

I thought back to the days when my children were born. I was so deliriously happy at each birth! My parents were the first ones I always called! How could Annie and Bret not call us? What kind of person was controlling their minds? How could Annie and Bret have fallen under a spell? Did they fear for their lives? Did they fear for their children's lives?

Are You out there God? Or do You live exclusively in that first world—the world I used to live in—the world that fell down? Do You ever visit the world I presently live in, God?

FEBRUARY 24, 1997

I spoke with Detective Charles today. He claimed that he had been busy with other things and had not yet begun his investigation into my daughter's Group. He told me he would get going on it the following week.

Again I wondered if he believed our story. Or did he just not have the energy or inclination to go forward?

FEBRUARY 25, 1997

Today was not a good day. I had a hard time getting out of bed. I had to make myself do what I needed to do—take a shower, get dressed, straighten up the house, do the laundry. Live. Breathe. Live. Act normal. Living life in a new world was not easy.

The phone call to Detective Charles yesterday had not helped. It only pushed me deeper into the darkness. I hated the darkness! I felt paralyzed in the darkness. I felt I could do nothing of consequence in the darkness. I was *nothing* in the darkness.

Invisible.

On the other hand, I loved the darkness. No one saw me in the shadows. No one knew me there. No one knew what I thought or felt in the darkness. I was invisible in that place. In the darkness I was hidden. Gone.

MARCH 1, 1997

How I wished things could be different. I have not gone out of the house for some time. I have not wanted to see anyone or talk to anyone. Words of sympathy have only angered me. The words have seemed hollow and without meaning. I have had to work so hard to appear normal when I am with others. And I get so tired. The truth of the matter is that I have barely been able to function. I have been too numb, too deep in the darkness. And I have not wanted anyone else to tell me to pray more. God was not listening. God had disappeared from me.

MARCH 2, 1997

I spoke with Carrie today. Nothing much has happened lately. Carrie has found out (from a former member), however, that no one in the group has been allowed to accept gifts from cut-off family members or friends. No surprise. Nothing about this group has surprised me for a very long time.

She told me that another "grandparent" has come forward with concerns about That Group. The grandparent told Carrie that her son, his wife, and their two children (10 and 13 years of age) are presently members of That Group. She also said that the thirteen-year-old claims she has been abused by some of the group members. This grandparent also stated that her son threatened to kill her if she reports anything to DCFS about the granddaughter's claims of abuse. She is very frightened for her grandchildren, and for herself as well.

MARCH 8, 1997

I had another dream last night. In this dream I had a conversation with Detective Charles. He asked me whether I wanted to raise my grandchildren or not. He told me that if I moved forward with the police and other authorities, someone might go after Annie and Bret. Perhaps the children would be taken away from them, and perhaps my relationship with them would be fatally damaged. I didn't know what to do!

MARCH 9, 1997

Liz and I went to see Detective Charles again. We spoke with him for about an hour. He still seemed to be distant and non-responsive for the most part. Is that what policemen are trained to do—show no emotion, no empathy, no interest? He did admit that he had not done much, although he did say he had spoken with the state's attorney and with some other police officers. He did say that he would continue to make more phone calls, and that he would like to interview members of That Group, if possible.

That is *not* going to happen. No way. The only way he would be able to interview any of them would be to arrest them first and then force them to be interviewed. But he has no hard evidence to make an arrest. So we all just keep spinning our wheels.

Poor Detective Charles is trying to help—but he doesn't have a clue what he is dealing with—neither do the state's attorney or any of the police officers in Detective Charles' department. I don't think DCFS has a clue either.

MARCH 13, 1997

A young woman named Trude (former Group member) spoke with Carrie. Trude believes that Ray (head preacher for That Group and brother to Bret) has gone over the edge. She explained that while he is preaching, he often crawls over the people he is preaching to—while they are seated in their chairs! And sometimes he pants and growls like a wild animal as he is moving about. Trude also said that he often has a terrified look on his face as he is crawling around. She wonders if he is making those faces on purpose in order to scare the people, or if he is terrified of something himself! One way or another, according to Trude, Ray is a frightening man!

MARCH 24, 1997

Liz and I met with Detective Charles again. He told us he had spoken with a few former members of That Group, but that they did not offer him any helpful information. Detective Charles related that the women he spoke with, in particular, seemed extremely nervous and frightened as they conversed. He said he would keep on trying.

But I doubted that Detective Charles would have any success with any former members. They would not talk much. I believe they were terrified that the leaders of That Group would hurt them in some way if they did. Detective Charles could try—but I believed they would never tell him much of anything.

After Liz and I left Detective Charles's office, we went over to an attorney's office (the daughter-in-law of Carrie). We spoke with her for about an hour. She encouraged us and told us that we were doing the right thing. But—between lines—indicated that the police work very slowly. She suggested we contact the FBI, or a private investigator. She gave us the name of a PI named Ted. She also suggested the name of another attorney who specialized in juvenile law. Finally, she suggested we contact a legislative person and try to get some laws changed regarding grandparent visitation rights. But she had no clue as to what we were up against. Neither did any of the people she suggested to us. No one could possibly know the situation unless they were actually living the horror of it all! But we could still try other avenues for help. It couldn't hurt.

We dared not give up!

APRIL 3, 1997

I spoke with a lawyer by the name of Dexter today. He must have thought I was a raving lunatic! I tried to tell him as much as I could about my daughter's situation, but the story is so complicated. He said that he needed time to digest it all. I did let him read Annie's letter. He said he wanted to show the letter to a forensic psychiatrist. He asked a lot of questions about Annie and Bret. None of our conversation seemed real. I began to think I was probably coming across as a very disturbed woman. But then, again, I *am* a very disturbed woman. This whole situation is *beyond* disturbing!

APRIL 4, 1997

More lights have been exploding! This time all around the outside of the church building where Al and I have worked as pastors for many years. Our building grounds have been vandalized several times of late. All of the outside lights along the ground have been knocked over and broken, and wires have been pulled out and bulbs smashed, etc. We had them fixed and then someone destroyed them again. My gut tells me that somebody strongly dislikes our church—or that someone strongly dislikes Al and me!

Should we have reported this to Dexter? To Detective Charles? To Detective Lawrence? Was the vandalism connected to That Group? It could have been. But we had no proof. It was reported to our local police department, and then we let it go.

APRIL 5, 1997

Al told me that a couple from our congregation received a letter from Annie and Bret. This couple had sent Annie and Bret a card congratulating them on the arrival of their new baby.

Apparently the card enraged Annie and Bret and they sent our friends a three-page letter full of anger and negativity towards us, saying we had put this couple "up to it," as far as they were concerned. Our friends made a copy of the letter and gave it to us. The letter was devastating!

APRIL 19, 1997

Dexter called. He decided he did not want to take our case. And I feel like Goldilocks in the three bears' house! I keep trying to find the right person to help us. But nothing seems to fit. And when I finally think I have found a fit, the bears come and chase me away. Why is this so hard?

MAY 1, 1997

Dexter called. He has decided to take our case!

MAY 8, 1997

I have had very little energy to do much of anything lately. I have felt totally drained. I have been thinking that it would be so much easier to give up and be swallowed by the darkness.

> *The cords of death entangled me; the anguish of the grave came upon me; I came to grief and sorrow. Then I called upon the name of the Lord: "Oh Lord, I pray you, save my life" (Psalm 116:3-4).*

MAY 25, 1997

Dexter came over to our house and spent about an hour with us. He explained that the cost of legal fees for our case would run about $10,000, with no guarantees. He said he would like to begin by hiring a "mole." Dexter said he wants to infiltrate That Group with this "mole" and find out what was going on. He wants to hire someone in his mid-twenties who has a military or law enforcement background. He said he had a forensic psychiatrist read Annie's letter, and the psychiatrist said Annie was way over the edge.

I also spoke with Liz today. She told me she has been hanging around the mall on Wednesday evenings, praying for the members of That Group. Apparently they all saw her last evening when they were leaving their church service, and they all ran to their cars and left the mall parking lot in a caravan. Jeze covered her face with her hands so that Liz could not see her face. What strange people!

MAY 26, 1997

Dexter called a detective service. He has tentatively hired a young white male in his mid-twenties—crew cut, muscular, and clean-shaven. This young man has been doing graduate work at the university. Dexter asked us to send him a retainer of $2,500.00 and we did. Interestingly, he said that his "mole" was a police detective, and it turns out that he knew both Ray and Bret. He went to high school with them. The "mole" said that Ray and Brett were both alcoholics and cocaine addicts, and that Ray had a history of violence.

JUNE 3, 1997

Kate, my sister Patty, and I are on our way to Oklahoma. Kate's biological Dad is very near death and on life support. Kate is beside herself.

Chapter 8

JUNE 7, 1997

Kate is with her father's family in Oklahoma. Patty and I are staying at a nearby hotel. Al called me from home and relayed that Liz had called Bret at his place of work so that she could get an address for Kate's Oklahoma family and send a sympathy card. Apparently Bret told her to get that information elsewhere and slammed down the phone.

The funeral is scheduled for Saturday. Annie and Bret will be arriving Friday night. I wonder what will happen when they come face-to-face with Kate. Friday is also little Rory's birthday. Will Rory remember Kate's face?

JUNE 9, 1997

Kate spent all day with her Oklahoma family. Her stepmother, Lynn, got out pictures of Rory and his little sister Bree for Kate to see. Why have Annie and Bret kept in touch with her biological father and new family, and not the rest of us? I don't understand at all.

JULY 10, 1997

Kate called me last night from her father's home.

She said that Annie and Bret had called earlier in the day and announced that Rory would not be coming to Oklahoma with them. What a huge disappointment! Lynn was planning to have a birthday party for Rory. Kate told me that Lynn felt sad and hurt. She didn't understand what was going on with them. Annie and Bret also made it very clear to Lynn that they would not be in the same room with Kate at any time. How sad. How cruel! The Dark One named Cruelty has infiltrated the minds of Annie and Bret. Sometime after that, Kate called again. Annie and Bret had arrived and they were furious that all of the pictures of their children were displayed in Lynn's house. Bret was also furious with Lynn's children over something, but Kate did not know what. Apparently Bret made a scene in front of all of them. Kate also said that she had yet to see Annie and Bret's new baby. They kept her veiled!

JULY 11, 1997

Kate called again, frantic at all of the strange things occurring. She said she had still not seen the baby as Bret and Annie were still keeping her veiled. No one had seen her face! Whenever she needed her diaper changed, Bret took her out to their car to change her. He refused to change her in the house!

Is any of this real? Am I dreaming? Is all of this bizarre behavior from Annie and Bret normal? Am I judging them too harshly? Is Kate making it all up on her end? Am I out of touch with reality? Is Kate out of touch with reality? Are we all living in an underworld of oddness, cruelty, and Dark Angels?

Al called me again. He said he had just spoken with Jason and Carrie. They had their court mediation with their son, Tom, regarding visitation rights with their grandchildren. Tom agreed to let his children see their grandparents for 2 hours each month. Jason and Carrie told the court that the arrangement was unacceptable. They would all go back to court.

Then Kate called again. Things did not go well at the memorial service. Annie and Bret totally ignored Kate, and no one was allowed to see the baby. They kept the baby veiled the entire time. They acted rudely towards everyone: they sat in their car for long periods of time, and they would not accept any gifts for the children. Bret told Kate to give all the gifts she brought for Rory to Goodwill. Kate's stepsister tried to get pictures of the baby but Annie and Bret would not allow it. Everyone was upset. Kate said she told Annie that she loved her. Annie ignored her. Annie and Bret left right after the memorial service and went back to their hotel saying that they would be back to Lynn's house in the morning—*after Kate leaves!*

JUNE 15, 1997

After a long week and a long trip, Kate, sister Patty, and I were finally back in our own homes. What an ordeal—the arrival of Annie and Bret without Rory, and with a *veiled* baby, and all the commotion at the memorial service and at their dead father's home. Is this how ordinary people lived their lives? With such contempt—with such viciousness? With such utter disregard for others?

Dexter called. He told us that the "mole" he hired has tried unsuccessfully to attend a Group worship service. The "Bouncer" with the gun is always standing guard at the door and does not allow anyone he does not know to enter. However, the "mole" was allowed to leave a note for Ray. I know Ray will not contact him, but I won't say that to Dexter, however. He would not believe me. Most of what I know, or sense about this strange little Group, is readily dismissed by those in authority who think they might be able to help, but in the end—can't.

Daughter Kate called. She relayed that she had just gotten off the phone with her stepsister. Apparently a big blowout had occurred on Sunday, the day after the memorial service, between Annie and Bret and the rest of the family. Apparently Annie and Bret continued to be outraged at Lynn for showing pictures of themselves and their children to Kate. They were also outraged that Kate had been allowed to sit with the family at the funeral. They screamed at Lynn, "How dare you let Kate sit with the family!" They also told Lynn and the rest of the family that they did not bring Rory with them because Kate was planning to kidnap him! And on the last day spent with their Oklahoma family, Annie and Bret *still* would not let anyone hold Bree, and they continued to keep her veiled. Kate's stepbrother walked out of the house in the middle of the verbal rampage. Then stepmom Lynn had "words" with Annie and Bret. Finally Annie and Bret walked out and drove back home. They never even said good-bye.

All of this has been too bizarre to take in. How could any of this have happened? And yet it did. Who would be able to comprehend it all? Who would believe our account? No one. Therefore I have decided to remain silent as to what happened down there. Kate and Annie's father got sick and died. They went down for his funeral. End of story. Nothing would be gained by revealing what really happened. The *truth* will continue to be veiled!

JUNE 15, 1997

I called Dexter thinking he would not believe my story of what had happened in Oklahoma. Actually, to my surprise, he seemed to believe me! Then, shock of all shocks, Dexter told me that Ray had called our "mole" and had asked the "mole" all kinds of questions. (Actually the "mole" relayed to Dexter that he had been "grilled" by Ray.) Dexter really wants our "mole" to get inside That Group so that he can get a better handle on what is going on. I told him I doubted that the "mole" would be able to get inside.

JUNE 19, 1997

Kate called. She had been on the phone with her stepsister again. Apparently the entire Oklahoma family was troubled by Annie and Bret's behavior.

They don't understand what has happened, but they all realize something is terribly wrong. Annie is not the same Annie they have known and loved over the years. The new Annie is rude, cruel, and a total stranger. On Sunday, before Annie and Bret left, Lynn got out all the old family pictures hoping something might jar Annie's memories of good times. Lynn brought out many pictures of Annie and Kate as little girls. But Annie was not the least bit interested in any of them. It is as if Annie is discounting her entire past—as if there is no past for her at all, only the present.

None of this makes any sense. What has happened to my child? To my beautiful daughter? Where has she gone? Will she ever return? I feel like I am in "Never Never Land," searching for a lost child.

Now I lay her down to sleep.
I pray Thee Lord, her soul to keep.
And if she dies before she wakes,
I pray Thee Lord, her soul to take.

JUNE 28, 1997

I spoke with Liz today. She sounded depressed and defeated. I wanted to tell her about Dexter and the "mole" he had hired to get inside That Group, but I decided not to. I didn't want to jeopardize the "mole's" work—or his safety. Besides, Dexter told us to keep silent about it.

During my conversation with Liz, she told me that the courts had granted Carrie and Jason one weekend every other month with their grandkids. I hoped the judgment would be of some help to the rest of us.

I had another nightmare last night. I was surrounded by evil beings. They were everywhere—taunting me, laughing at me, and getting up into my face. And they were so angry with me! I just stood there, terrified, unable to move. When will these nightmares end?

JULY 11, 1997

I had yet another nightmare! I dreamed about rats—big rats. They were running everywhere! The rats were attacking me, biting me, and they were eating up my beloved pet dog. I tried to kill them. I hit them and hit them and hit them. But they would not die. They *would not* die! Why wouldn't they die?

The nightmares I have been having pale to the "daymares" I am having! Kate called again and relayed to me that while Annie was in Oklahoma, she told her father's family that Kate had punched her in the abdomen when she was 9 months pregnant with Rory—that she had tried to kill Rory! Where does Annie come up with this stuff? She has totally gone off the edge!

JULY 17, 1997

Dexter called. Once again, our "mole" has not been able to get inside That Group. Interestingly, Ray called our "mole's" roommate one evening and grilled him! After that conversation both our "mole" and his roommate became frightened. Dexter told me that he is convinced That Group is a hate group. Dexter also told me that he is going to station some investigators outside the building where That Group meets on Wednesday nights. They want to see who goes in and who goes out and what cars they get into. Dexter is also thinking about assigning a female operative to the case to see if she can get inside. I don't think she will get inside either. That Group won't let anyone new inside.

AUGUST 23, 1997

Nothing new. I really want to call Dexter; I haven't heard from him in weeks. I wish he would keep us more informed! We are paying him! Yet we wait and wait for his phone calls. Any news—good or bad—is better than no news at all. I just don't get it. Why can't he give us updates? At least weekly! It sure isn't like the movies when the detectives work closely with their clients.

Actually, I haven't heard from *any* of my contacts for *some time* regarding any news at all about That Group. This is definitely not like the movies at all. CSI can get all crimes solved in an hour. Why can't real life situations work at least a little bit faster? Has everyone just given up? Why the silence? There are little children who *need* our help. Little children who are suffering at the hands of the adult members of this group. Doesn't anyone care about the children? What about You God? Do You care?

Now I lay them down to sleep:
I pray thee Lord their souls to keep.
And if they die before they wake,
I pray thee Lord their souls to take.

AUGUST 25, 1997

Finally! Some news! But it isn't good news. Carrie called me. She said that Tom's children had visited with her and her husband. She relayed that the children looked very thin and had unhealthy looking complexions, and that while the children hungrily gobbled up all of the food that she offered them at mealtimes, Paulie mentioned more than once that they often were fed only mashed potatoes or noodles for meals. Carrie also noticed that the children wore ill-fitting clothes and shoes. And she said when Tom dropped off the children, and again when he picked them up, his eyes looked vacant, his face expressionless—blank.

I wish she would call DCFS and tell them what she has observed! Maybe she thinks DCFS won't believe her. Maybe she doesn't want to jeopardize their visitation rights. Is there a code of silence that she has to adhere to? Are family reputations on the line? Does she fear for her safety if she goes to the authorities? Or the safety of the children?

Grayson also called. He told me he was keeping an eye on That Group—who goes in and who goes out—men, women, and children. He said that during their meetings, everything is closed up tight and there is very little light filtering out from behind the closed shades. The meetings take place at night and often go on for several hours at a time. Grayson has told me much of this before. But it is still good to hear from him—even if the news is not good.

Grayson told me months ago that he and the police would be working together—that they had a plan in place to investigate That Group—that they did not think That Group was a healthy group for children to be involved with. Are they implementing their plan? Are the children safe—or not? If they believe the children are NOT safe, why isn't something being done? Are they afraid of something? Their jobs? Their families? If the children are safe, they would say so and that would be that. But they have not told me that the children are safe. So I believe that they are not. Why won't someone help the children? Is it so impossible? Does no one want to know the truth about the children? Is it better for the children if we all just keep silent? I have no answers. And I'm not sure if I have a God.

Are You out there God? Is there no one You can send to find out what is happening to the children? Is there no one You can send who is unafraid to speak for the children?

SEPTEMBER 5, 1997

Liz called me with some startling news. She found out that Will and Justine and their two children had defected from That Group! Apparently they wrote a long letter of apology to their former pastor and began to attend their former church once again. Will and Justine stated That Group was not a safe place for children.

They said that they would not go to the authorities, however. They believed if they did, the leaders of That Group would punish them. Perhaps, even kill them! And so the code of silence continues. No one is brave enough to help the children still inside. The Dark Ones named Intimidation, Fear, and Silence prevail! Is there no one brave enough to fight them? Liz also told me she found out that a man (whose son was involved with That Group) broke inside their space during one of their meetings and found all of the members (men, women, and children) sitting in semi-darkness, on hard backed chairs, in a trance-like state. He dragged his son on out. Liz does not know the name of the father or the son. I wonder if this particular father would be willing to go to the authorities. *Dear God help these children!*

SEPTEMBER 8, 1997

The nightmares have begun again—three of them in a row! In the first dream I found myself trudging up a steep hill. Extreme pain radiated from my left leg as I was climbing, as if I was carrying a heavy load of some kind over my left shoulder. A huge spider web loomed at the top of the hill—a web the size of a large building. I did not want to go there but I kept on climbing. In fact, I could not stop climbing. When

I reached the top of the hill I tried to go around the web, but I got caught in it instead. I screamed and thrashed at the sticky strands that were suffocating me. I finally managed to get out, leaving the heavy load I was carrying still in the web. I stumbled my way back down the hill, terrified that the web would come after me.

In the second dream, I found myself outside of my house with a broom in my hands, frantically sweeping away spider webs—thousands of them! I came across a very large web and I could not sweep it away or pull it down. It was too strong. I got caught up in the web. A huge spider came out of the web and fell in my hair—then it moved to my shoulder. I tried to bat it away. As I batted at it, the thing stared at me with its huge red eyes. I screamed for help, and someone came and swept the web and the spider off of me. I didn't know who it was. I did not see his face.

The third dream was not about spiders. I dreamed that Annie and Bret came home. They were tense and skittish, but they were happy to see me; I was so happy to see them. But they did not bring the children. Where were the children? Had they left them behind? Where were the children?

SEPTEMBER 13, 1997

I heard from Liz. She said that she had sat in a borrowed car outside of That Group's space a few nights ago. She had wanted to see her grown children and her grandchildren. She disguised herself and sat in a borrowed car—waiting for them to come out of the mall. Is this what it has come to? Does she have to spy on her children and grandchildren to get a glimpse of them while they pass by? This whole situation is out of control! This just can't be happening. It is all wrong. Liz has to be making it up! But she isn't.

SEPTEMBER 14, 1997

I dreamed of Annie last night. In my dream she came to me and apologized for her behavior. She was crying. Her blouse was open and I saw wounds on her chest—all in neat rows—blood still coming out from them. Was this the price she must pay for defecting? She was alone. Did she have to leave the children behind? Was this dream a message to me? Am I wanting too much from her? Do I just need to let her go?

I wish I could understand what all of my dreams mean. Do they mean anything at all? Or are they just dreams made up in my own mind? I don't know. I don't know if I will ever know. I wish all of these strange dreams would go away.

NOVEMBER 9, 1997

I had another strange dream last night. Evil came to me. Stared me in the face. Dark. Frightening. Menacing. It wanted to destroy me. I told it to go away. I reached out and touched it and tried to push it away. I screamed and screamed at it. I woke up when Al began to shake me out of the dream. Al comforted me for a long time, and he prayed for me. Eventually

I went back to sleep when I felt safe again. When would these dreams end? What did they mean? How could I remain sane with these recurring nightmares invading my mind?

LATE 1997

I met a woman who believes that I am in the middle of a spiritual battle with the members of That Group. She believes that there is much evil in this strange group, and it has a firm grip on all its members. She believes I have to fight the Dark Ones. She believes that God will give me the strength to destroy them; I don't believe that I can do anything of the sort. God has not been around to help. Why would God suddenly appear now? I am tired. Weary. Physically, mentally, and spiritually, I feel washed out. I can hardly get out of bed in the mornings. I am ready to give up. I am far too weak to fight, and no one wants to help. Not one person with firsthand knowledge of what is going on is willing to speak to the authorities! The silence is deafening!

Perhaps this is the greatest evil of all: those who know firsthand what is going on will not tell the authorities what they know! And I am about ready to go over to that silent side myself. It would be so much easier; I don't have any hard evidence anyway. I have only second- and thirdhand information. No one takes me seriously. Perhaps those who know the truth would rather I let it all go. Maybe I should call it a day. I just can't keep doing this!*God seems very far away, and the Dark Ones are breathing down the back of my neck. Help me God! Help the children!* The woman I met who told me I was in a spiritual battle suggested I read from Jeremiah 31:15-17:

> *This is what the Lord says:*
> *"A voice is heard in Ramah,*
> *Mourning and great weeping.*
> *Rachel weeping for her children*
> *And refusing to be comforted,*
> *Because her children are no more."*
>
> *This is what the Lord says:*
> *"Restrain your voice from weeping,*
> *And your eyes from tears,*
> *For your work will be rewarded.*
> *They will return from the land of the*
> *enemy.*
> *So there is hope in your future.*
> *Your children will return to their own*
> *land."*

But when, Lord God? When will they return? I mourn for my children and grandchildren day and night. I cannot control my grieving. I am inconsolable. I cannot be comforted. I have little hope that my children and grandchildren will ever return . . . If only my faith were as strong as the prophet Jeremiah's faith. Then perhaps I would not struggle so. Then perhaps I could be comforted. Then perhaps I could have hope. God, You seem to have forgotten me. You seem to have forgotten all of the families who have lost their children and grandchildren to this group. God, You seem to have forgotten the littlest lambs in Your fold. Why, God . . . ?

This woman also recommended Psalm 46:10: *"Be still and know that I am God."* Then she spoke these words to me: "Don't look back. Don't look forward. Look only up."

But I doubt that this advice will work for me. God is absent. I call out to Him and He is not there. I "look up" and He is not there . . .

We decided to release Dexter. He was not getting anywhere. He was not communicating anything hopeful to us. I am so disappointed in him. Why couldn't he have found a way to rescue the children? Where are we to go from here?

> *Restrain your voice from weeping, and*
> *your eyes from tears, for your work will*
> *be rewarded. They will return from the*
> *land of the enemy. So there is hope in your*
> *future. Your children will return to their*
> *own land (Jeremiah 31:16-17).*

EARLY 1997

I miss my daughter and her family so much. Will I ever see them again? Will there ever be a place for us? Somehow? Somewhere?

APRIL 3, 1997

Grayson called! I spoke with him at length. He told me that the members of That Group have been very rude to him. He said he received a nasty three-page letter from them, condemning him and his foundation for "sins committed against us." That Group demanded that Grayson repent! They accused Grayson of four sins:

> Parking in their parking spaces in the back of the building.

> Stealing chairs from them.

> Music playing too loudly on Wednesday evenings.

> Music playing too loudly on Saturday evenings.

Grayson told me that members of That Group have actually stormed into the middle of Grayson's worship services ranting and raving about the sins that Grayson's foundation has committed against them.

On another note, Grayson also told me that Carrie needs to call DCFS regarding Paulie's bed-wetting and his habit of pulling down his pants whenever he thinks he has done something bad—(so that he can be spanked). Carrie will not call the authorities, however. She will not chance upsetting their son Tom. They will not chance upsetting their visitation rights with their grandchildren. She has told me so. The Dark One named Fear is totally in control of her!

Carrie and Jason are not able to help with anything at this point. They want to protect their family, so they dare not go against That Group. They are afraid, and I understand. Carrie and Jason's silence buys them time to be with their grandchildren. But I wonder if they can sleep at night . . .

Please God! Please send someone to help the children!

Chapter 9

EARLY FALL OF 1998

The last conversation between Grayson and me happened months ago. Nothing at all has happened since. In the meantime, the rest of us continue to live and breathe as best as we can in the new world we have created for ourselves. Our youngest daughter finished high school, graduating in the top 10% of her class. She went to the prom in the spring, and she was awarded all kinds of honors at her graduation—academically, as well as athletically and musically. Presently she is enrolled in a small private university where she is doing well. Our oldest daughter is at a state university and is also doing well. Life continues for all of us . . . but it will never be the way it was before that Terrible Day When The Sky Turned Black . . .

OCTOBER, 1998

I often dream of unfolding my little sparrow wings and flying to the beautiful garden. Such nice wings:

small, but dependable. And while in the garden I can hear that voice from deep inside of me—that voice I have heard before. From the back of my mind. From the top of a very high shelf—long forgotten, full of dust and spider webs.

That voice sometimes scolds me, especially when I feel weak and insignificant. It tells me to buck up. To not give up. To not give in. And when I tell that voice that I can't go on, that voice tells me I need to think about the children.

That voice is determined to keep the truth in front of me. It is determined to keep my family in front of me. It tells me it is keeping all of my memories in a Memory Box. And all of my unshed tears in a Tear Box . . . in case I need the memories one day. In case I need the tears one day. I don't know who this voice belongs to, or why it says what it says.

I like sitting in my beautiful garden. It is sunny and warm there. And quiet—except for the rustling of small animals hiding underneath the flowers and in the branches of the fruit trees. Sometimes in the quietness of the garden, I think I feel God's presence. Calm. Soothing.

Maybe God is here is after all.

Carrie, Jason, Liz, Al, and I all went to court

today in support of our friend Leah, whose son, Stan, has accused her of stalking his family. He had her arrested because she was sitting (in her car) in the parking lot of the strip mall that houses That Group. Leah's husband was also in court to support her—as well as her arresting officer. The officer did not like that he had to arrest her.

It was quite a scene in the courtroom. Everyone got riled up as Stan took the witness stand and spewed out hatred toward his mother, accusing her of harassment and stalking. And at the end of the session? The judge put a two-year restraining order on Leah. What a sad day!

Why couldn't the judge see through the sham? Was he afraid, too? Had the judge succumbed to the same code of silence that all the others had succumbed to? Was he keeping silent in exchange for his own safety? Did he fear for the safety of *his* family? Did he *know* what was at stake? Had the Dark Angels named Fear, Deceit, Dismissal, and Denial taken over the courtroom? Were there no limits to their power? Were there no spaces where they could not go? After court, Liz, Carrie, Al, and I went out to lunch with Grayson and his assistant, Bill. And after we filled them in on what had just happened at court, Grayson and Bill had a few new things to report:

Grayson said that all of the members of That Group are now escorted from their cars to their worship services inside of the mall. The "bouncer" does all of the escorting. I wonder if the High Priestess thinks that her members will run if they are not under her control at all times? I wonder if she is afraid that someone or something is after them? I wonder if that is why she has her members lock the doors after everyone is inside their space? I wonder if that is why they lower all the shades on their windows before they begin their meetings? I wonder if that is why they worship in the dark?

Then Bill relayed the group has changed the locks on the doors of their meeting space—both front and back. And Bill found out that they did this without consulting their landlord! According to Bill, the landlord is not happy about it! Again, what are the group members afraid of? Are there Dark Creatures breathing down their necks? Is a Dark One whispering in Jeze's ear? Are the Dark Ones filling up their worship space?

According to Bill, That Group has also set up a video cam so that all people walking in the hall just outside their doors can be seen. Are they afraid that Dark Ones are wandering in the hallway? Do they know that perhaps the Prince of Darkness is swirling in their own gathering space behind their own locked doors? After our lunch with Grayson and Bill, Liz and I paid a visit to a man named Rob. He had been a member of That Group for a time, but he had recently left. His experience had not been a good one, and he wanted to tell us about some of the troubling things he had witnessed inside That Group. Liz and I were really surprised that he wanted to talk to us.

First of all, he told us that a former member of That Group had recently killed himself. Rob believes the suicide was directly related to something that happened in That Group, but he can't prove it. It would seem that not only are the members terrified of Dark Ones, they are also terrified of each other! He also told us that all adult members of That Group are required to give the lion's share of all they earn to their group. He said he had nothing left; That Group took everything he had—his wife, his money—everything.

He then explained to us that Ray claims he is God, and that all must bow to him. Even so, Rob stated that Ray looks to Jeze for orders; he can do nothing apart from her. But I wonder how Ray can claim to be God? There is NO sign of God in him at all, or in any of these people. God is not cruel; God is not manipulative. He doesn't cause fear. These people are not worshiping God! But then who are they worshiping?

Rob told us that, at times, married couples are split up during worship services. The sheep (the righteous ones) sit on one side while the goats (the sinners) sit on the other side. Therefore a married couple could be split up accordingly. If the couple is split up during worship, they are not allowed any contact until the goat is purged of his or her sins and welcomed back in with the sheep. During this time of no contact, the couple cannot speak to each other, cannot eat with one another, and cannot have sex together. The "no contact" order sometimes goes on for days or even weeks.

Jeze directs everything. She tells her people when to marry and when to divorce. She tells them when to have children. She controls their mail and their phone calls. She controls where they work and where their children attend school—if at all. (Many of the children are home-schooled.) She also controls what her people wear and how they comb their hair. And she tells them what businesses they can frequent and what businesses they can't. She also controls their money, and she tells them how to discipline their children. She is the one who told them all that *they had to break contact with all of their former family members and their former friends*! She totally controls her members' lives! And I wonder why they allow her to control their lives?

Then Rob told us that Ray has physically, mentally, and spiritually abused little Rory, and that Annie and Bret have done nothing to stop it. Also, Ray allows his own children to taunt Rory. Ray claims that *his* children are the "chosen ones." Little Rory is Ray's "scapegoat" and is punished often. Little Rory is also frequently told that his grandparents are "bad." Ray has also told Rory many times that he (Rory) is "bad."Rob said no one ever challenges Ray or Jeze—especially Jeze! She is in total control of all her members, and she has chosen Ray as her successor. She has told the members that no one, except Ray, is allowed to interpret Scripture. My guess is that Jeze is also trying to control God!

Rob's words flowed on and on. According to Rob, Ray repeatedly browbeats my daughter, and she is constantly in trouble. Rob believes that Annie wants "out," but in order to leave she would have to leave Bret and her children. This statement from Rob is both good news and bad news. The good news is that she wants out. The bad news is that she won't leave without her children, so she won't leave. My heart cries out for her—all of me cries out for her. Will she forever be held hostage? And there isn't a thing I can do about it. There isn't a thing anyone can do about it as long as former group members do not go to the authorities and make complaints!

Then Rob explained to us that vile curses are regularly hurled at the homes of extended family members of That Group, and that "death prayers" are often prayed for extended family members.

He said that all members who have left That Group were regularly in trouble (while they were still in the group). Ray liked to punish those who sinned by threatening to beat them up; no wonder they left! Still, none of them have gone to the authorities. They are too afraid.

Rob also told us that at one point in time, Jeze proclaimed that when children reach the age of three they are accountable for their actions and should be severely punished for their transgressions.

Finally Rob said to us that he was prepared to go

to the police but he would *never* testify in court about any of what he had just told us. And I wondered how that could be possible. If he told the police everything, wasn't there a possibility he might need to testify in court on behalf of the children? If so, how would he not have to go to court? Would he mysteriously disappear? What was he so afraid of, other than the fact that his wife has threatened to kill him if he left That Group? He *has* left That Group! He is already living in fear that she will show up at his house with a gun! Is there someone else out there besides his wife who wants him dead?

Liz and I left our meeting with Rob shaken and terrified for our grown children and grandchildren. But what could we do? How could we help them? We were encouraged, however, that Rob told us he would go to the police!

OCTOBER 21, 1998

I called yet another attorney today; his name is Rudy. I told him about That Group: about what Rob told us, about Grayson, and about the children who needed to be rescued. I don't think he believed a word of what I told him. He did say, however, that he would call Grayson. Perhaps he wanted to know from Grayson if my story was credible.

OCTOBER 25, 1998

I called Carrie. She gave me the name of a private investigator that her husband's law firm has used for years. His name is Ted. I also called Rob and left a message on his answering machine, thanking him for talking to us. I told him Grayson would like to speak with him, and that I hoped they could meet soon.

OCTOBER 26, 1998

Rob called and left a message on my machine. He said he would be willing to speak with Grayson. I feel very, very good about that!

OCTOBER 28, 1998

Bill, Grayson's assistant, called and told me that Grayson and Rob were planning to get together soon to talk. Then Bill asked me why some of the others who had left That Group had not gone to the police. He asked me if I thought they were all afraid of something. I told Bill that I believed they were all, indeed, afraid of something or someone!

NOVEMBER 1, 1998

I spoke with our new lawyer, Rudy, and a really bizarre thing happened! He told me I should hire a private investigator and gave me the name of Ted. Rudy said Ted had worked with him for a number of years. What a weird coincidence! This is the same Ted that works for Carrie's husband and her lawyer daughter! Ted must be a really good detective—or something else is going on! Something other worldly!

NOVEMBER 2, 1998

I called Ted and spoke with him for a long time.

He must have thought I was a real screwball because he told me he was not interested in taking the case. I will have to get another name . . .

NOVEMBER 3, 1998

I had another nightmare. It was complicated; it was like a warning of some sort. But then who gets warnings in dreams anymore? In the dream, two sets of people were fighting against each other. I did not recognize anyone except for Annie. I saw her only briefly—her small face white—her body language looking frightened and helpless. Apparently I had befriended the leader of one of these sets of people. I thought it might be Rob, but I wasn't sure. But somehow I had befriended one of the leaders—and then I betrayed him. The situation was not good. A fierce battle ensued. A woman kept screaming at me and berating me.

There were lots of people holding guns, big guns. I heard someone yell, "Shoot!" I found myself begging Rob for forgiveness. Begging him to let me live! Begging him to take me back into his confidence. He refused. He was so angry at me and called me a traitor!

NOVEMBER 4, 1998

Al and I went to an evening worship service at Rob's new church at Rob's invitation. The building was very small. The service reminded me of the little church where Annie and Bret had gotten married a lifetime ago, only the atmosphere was friendlier, more comfortable.

Besides Rob, we saw many of the others who had defected from That Group. We also met a man from Georgia named Dr. Martin who was the guest preacher for the evening. They were all so friendly to us! I could hardly believe that any of them had ever been mixed up with That Group. In fact, they all talked to us about That Group after the service and expressed their concerns for the children and all of the others still inside. One man actually used the word "cult" when describing That Group. And my question is still the same: Why don't any of these people go to the police? *Where are the heroes? Apparently, being a hero is not easy . . .*

DECEMBER 4, 1998

Liz and I decided to be "spies" for an evening so that we could get a glimpse of our children and grandchildren. Thankfully, Grayson gave us a key to his office and we had his permission to enter. His space was still located right next to That Group's space. Now we would be able to see them from inside the mall instead of outside from the parking lot. We dressed in dark clothes, baseball hats, and sunglasses before we left Liz's house, and then we drove to the mall.

We entered Grayson's office through the rear door. It was pitch black inside, and the silence was overwhelming. Even though Grayson had given us permission to do this, we felt like criminals lurking in the shadows.

Cautiously and quietly we moved to the front of the office where some light spilled in through the windows and the glass door separating the main hallway of the mall from Grayson's office. Once we were in front, even though it was still fairly dark, we decided to keep all of the inside lights off, lest someone happening by in the mall corridor think something suspicious was occurring inside. Once our eyes adjusted to the semi-darkness, the light from the hallway was enough for us to see.

We began to settle in. I checked my little tape recorder to make sure it was in working order; it was. I hoped we would be able to use it by putting it up to the wall between Grayson's office space and That Group's space. We wanted to hear for ourselves what went on during their worship service. We believed that with all of the curses and death threats being hurled at us, we deserved to hear it ourselves—firsthand. Next we checked inside our purses and took out paper and pens tucked inside them so that we could take notes. Then we crouched low to the ground just beneath the windows, tried to get in somewhat comfortable positions, and waited for them to appear.

And all the while, my heart banged mercilessly against the inside wall of my chest. What were we going to see? Were they coming tonight? Would we get a glimpse of our children and grandchildren? What if they saw our car parked in the back of the parking lot?

Would they all turn around and go home? Would they call the police? Had their "High Priestess," perhaps, used her "supernatural powers" to sniff out our plans and warn her followers?

We waited and waited. Then, in the flick of the wrist, they were there—walking down the hallway—escorted by a very big man with a menacing face. But we could not see any other faces! They were all bundled up from head to toe in coats, hats, mittens, and boots. And they were walking so quickly. In the blink of an eye, it was all over. They filed past our window and into their gathering place, where the door was quickly shut behind them and the blinds were tightly drawn. End of our stakeout—end of our opportunity. All we were left with was great sorrow that we had been unable to see any of their faces.

However, we still had our little tape recorder, so we made our way to the wall that separated Grayson's office space from That Group's space. We pressed our recorder to the wall and listened—our ears right on the wall, but there was no sound. No sound at all save a little shuffling around of furniture. Nothing for our small tape recorder to record. Nothing!

We waited for about an hour. Finally, we decided to leave, and we snuck out the back door. So much for our spy plans. We left the mall parking lot feeling like a pair of very foolish grandmothers who didn't have a clue as to how to reach their children and grandchildren.

Chapter 10

DECEMBER 9, 1998

Al and I went to see our new lawyer, Rudy. We spoke with him at great length, but his bottom line was this: "I can't help you unless you get me some hard evidence." We left his office feeling crestfallen and weary. We had no firsthand hard evidence. We felt like no one was going to be able to help us.

JANUARY 18, 1999

I received a call from Liz with some startling information. She told me Leah had just called her and said that her son, Stan, daughter-in-law, Shelley, and their two teenaged boys had been kicked out of That Group.

The thought that immediately ran through my head was that Stan was the same man who, a few years ago, had taken his mom to court and accused her of stalking him and his family. However, at the present, Stan and Shelley were living with his parents, Leah and John. What strange twists and turns this story takes!

Also, Leah relayed to Liz that the two teenaged boys were in trouble with the law for stealing, and they were being held in a juvenile detention facility. In addition, DCFS was also involved with their parents, as the boys claimed their parents had abused them. The boys told the police that their parents were in the habit of stripping their clothes off of them the minute they got home from school, and then padlocking them in their bedroom, which they shared. The boys had been caught molesting each other. The Darkness had found its way into their home.

Stan and Shelley are pointing their fingers at Jeze! They believe she is the cause of the boys' troubling behavior. Stan and Shelley unloaded lots of information to John and Leah about That Group, including the fact that the members regularly drove by the homes of their parents and grandparents and hurled out curses and prayers for their deaths! Of course we already knew that, but now we have additional confirmation of these activities going on. Would Stan and Shelley go to the police about these activities? I doubted it. I believed that they were afraid of Jeze, just as all of the others were.

JANUARY 20, 1999

I was on the phone all morning. Bill, Grayson's assistant, called and relayed a very strange incident that had happened on Sunday, the day before, in the mall corridor just outside of That Group's space. Bill told me that he never worked on Sundays, but for some reason he felt an urge to go to his office that afternoon. When he got there, he came upon a very small boy sitting in the hall just outside of That Group's space. The boy was alone and appeared to be in some kind of trance. The boy was facing the wall, not moving at all—just sitting and staring at the wall. Bill could hear some voices inside of That Group's space, so he figured they were having one of their Sunday afternoon meetings and that the little boy was being punished for some random sin.

Four hours later, when Bill left his office, the little boy was still sitting in the hall, alone, trance-like, and staring at the wall. Bill became very concerned for the boy and returned to his office to call the local police department.

The supervisor of that police department, Officer Hetrick, arrived shortly thereafter to speak with the boy and with Bill. The police officer knocked on the door of That Group's space and asked to speak with the boy's mother. The boy's mother spoke with the officer and took the boy inside. The police officer told her that there would be an investigation done by DCFS!

At approximately 6:00p.m. that Sunday, Bill finally left his office. As he entered the corridor of the mall, several members of That Group appeared and yelled out at him, "You can run, but you cannot hide!" Bill left the building feeling shaken—as if he had encountered a band of Satan's demons!

After I finished speaking on the phone with Bill that morning, I immediately called the local DCFS field office and asked for the supervisor. I spoke with a Mr. Nolan and expressed my concern for the children involved with That Group. I told him that I was aware of the incident with the little boy on Sunday and that both the local police and DCFS had been contacted about the situation. Mr. Nolan did not give me much of a response. He simply told me to call the "hotline" in Springfield. But I did not. I had already done that before and had received no response from them either.

Don't any of these people want to help kids? Have they all been seduced by the darkness? It would seem so. Carrie and I decided to see Detective Charles later in the week and find out what he knew about the situation.

JANUARY 22, 1999

Liz, Carrie, and I met with Detective Charles. We had quite a bit of new information to give him, including the situation with Stan and Shelley's two boys and the boys' court hearing coming up in February. Detective Charles said that he was not aware of the boys' case and that the other police department must have taken the report.

Twin Cities and Twin Police Departments, separated by only a few miles, and they can't communicate with each other? Even though current group members, former members, *and* families of both current and former group members are scattered throughout both of the cities and both of the police department jurisdictions, the two departments can't get together and compare their notes?

Detective Charles told us that he would contact

the other department to get some information. I am willing to bet he will not. I am sure he would rather not deal with us. Detective Charles has had, and continues to have, ample opportunity to talk with a number of people concerning this group—including the other PD, the local DCFS, (which serves both cities), and the school officials where Stan and Shelley's boys attend. Something is so wrong here!

There are also many others that Detective Charles could be interviewing, including Evin and Bella, Rob, Dr. Martin, Grayson, Bill, or our lawyers Dexter or Rudy. Maybe he has already spoken to some of them, but I don't really know. If he has, he hasn't said anything to us about it. I just don't know if Detective Charles really wants to help us!

I wish Leah would come forward with her information about Stan and Shelley and their two boys. Leah told Liz that Shelley was a "river of information" concerning all that is going on at That Group. It would be great if Stan or Shelley would come forward themselves! Or if only the mother of that little boy found sitting alone for four hours in the mall corridor would step up. I just wish *someone* would come forward with firsthand information and contact the police! I wish *someone* would light a fire under Detective Charles.

I mailed a letter to Dr. Martin; I don't know what his response will be, but I definitely think he knows more about That Group than he lets on. I sense he is afraid of something. Perhaps he can see the darkness growing. In the letter, I told him I was ready to go to the press with everything I knew about That Group. (Although I wasn't sure the press printed information unless it was firsthand information.)

I spoke with Liz. She has visited with Leah again. Leah told Liz that they (Leah, John, Stan, Shelley, and the boys) had gone Christmas shopping together, and during the shopping outing, Stan told his mother that he loved her and had dropped the restraining order against her. However, all that being said, Leah told Liz that her relationship with all of them was very strained. She said the two boys were never let out of their parents' sight, and that the boys even had to ask permission to use the bathroom when needed. Leah also relayed to Liz that she had called the boys' school and asked school officials why it had taken them months to notify the parents that there had been a problem with the boys' behavior.

Why have these school officials been so reticent about helping these boys? What are they so afraid of? Can they feel the Darkness breathing down their necks? Can they smell the Dark Ones nearby? But I would be afraid too. The Destroyers are very fierce, and there are legions of them! No one wants to rattle their cages! Cowards!

Leah also told Liz that the boys' court hearing was scheduled for February 26. The charges were theft (for both boys) and child molestation (for acts committed by the older boy on the younger boy).

The Dark Ones continue to circle their prey.

And the heroes run away.

FEBRUARY 3, 1999

Rob called me and was very upset. He said that Dr. Martin had received my letter and was unhappy that I might send my story to the newspaper. Dr. Martin called Evin about the situation. Evin called Rob. And finally, Rob called me. They were all very unhappy with me. I told Rob that I didn't really want to contact the newspaper, but no one seemed willing to help the children inside That Group, and I didn't know what else to do.

Finally, Rob told me he *would* go to the police with all the information he knew about That Group. (Apparently he would rather go to the police than for the story to be in the newspaper, even though the newspaper would probably not print the story anyway.) Rob said he planned to go talk to Detective Charles sometime in the next 24 hours. Interestingly, Rob also told me that he had a twin brother who had been a police officer in the other police department—Twin Cities—Twin Police Departments—twin brothers. How strange is that? And neither of the departments seemed to know what the other was doing!

Rob told me he was ready to make a full statement to the Police, and also said he was willing to speak with my lawyer. Then he apologized to me for all of my suffering, and for the sufferings of all the families who had children and grandchildren involved with That Group. I accepted his apology and told him that we have indeed all suffered, and that it was time for the pain to end. He agreed, and explained that he had thought God would bring it all to an end, which is why he hadn't come forward yet.

Why hasn't God come forward? Why hasn't God brought it all to an end?

Rob asked me if I thought the police would arrest him for being an "accessory" to the crimes committed against the children. I said I didn't know. But I told him that I was afraid he might hurt himself now that the truth was going to come out. He said he would not. He said he was already hurt. Then I told him I knew all about the death threats toward us. I also told him about the situation with the two boys and the upcoming court date set for them. I relayed to him the incident about the little boy in the mall corridor, and that the police, as well as DCFS, had been called in to investigate. Finally, I relayed to him that our county sheriff was also aware of all of the death threats and was on alert!

If Rob carries through with what he has told me, That Group may crumble, and Rob may become a hero. But he also might get himself killed! Being a hero is not easy.

Dear God give Rob courage. It won't be easy for him to be a hero and do what he said he would do!

FEBRUARY 4, 1999

I woke up feeling energized and full of hope after having had the conversation with Rob. Maybe it would be the day Rob would go to the police! Maybe it would be the day that would be the beginning of the end for That Group! I decided I should call both Rudy and Detective Charles about my conversation with Rob. I wanted to make sure they would be ready for whatever fallout might come of Rob's confession. As it turned out, however, neither man was in his office, so I left messages. Disappointed, I prayed that this was not a bad omen.

I brushed off my disappointment and decided to call Grayson's office. He was not in either; but Bill was, so I spoke with him a bit. It turned out to be an interesting conversation to say the least. Bill told me that he and Grayson had received a nasty letter from That Group, again! The leaders were furious that Bill had called the police and DCFS about the little boy in the mall corridor. Bill also told me that he ran into one of the members in the mall corridor a few days ago. The young man had glared fiercely at Bill, and Bill had felt overpowered by the hatred he saw in the young man's eyes.

God help us all! Where does this hateful power come from? How can it be so strong that others cower in fear before it?

I told Bill about the letter I had sent to Dr. Martin and about my conversation with Rob. Bill was amazed that Rob said he would go to the police and spill it all! Bill, too, is hopeful that Rob's "confession" might be the beginning of the end for That Group.

Later in the day I spoke with Dr. Martin. He told

me that it was he who advised Rob to go to the police with any and all information about That Group. Dr. Martin advised Rob to get a lawyer before he made his statement. He went on to tell me that he had a conversation with Evin, and that Evin had admitted to him that he had witnessed many of the children in That Group stand in corners for hours at a time as punishment for various sins committed.

Then came the final zinger! Dr. Martin told me that Rob had repented of his fascination with child pornography! I wondered what would become of Rob if he confessed that to the police; I could only imagine that his lawyer would tell him to keep his mouth shut. I couldn't help but wonder if he had taken pictures of any of the children in That Group. This was getting uglier and uglier!

Detective Charles finally returned my call late in the afternoon. He said that Rob had left a message for him and said he was ready to talk. I thanked God that it was finally happening! It would soon be over! Soon the Dark Ones would be exposed—and flee!

FEBRUARY 7, 1999

I made a lot of phone calls. First of all, I spoke with my lawyer, Rudy. I told him about all of the new information I had received in the past few days. Rudy's calm voice told me he was optimistic but cautious. He told me to keep after Detective Charles. He also told me that it would not hurt to call DCFS again. The last thing he said to me was rather alarming. He told me to write everything down and put all of my notes in a safe place—in case anything would happen to me. Did he believe that Jeze would order one of her henchmen to kill me?

Next, I called Bill. He was very happy that the group could soon unravel. He told me I ought to turn up the heat—that I should write another letter to Dr. Martin and ask him to come clean with all he knows about That Group. That's easy for Bill to suggest; I am afraid to write another letter.

Then Bill told me something that practically knocked me over. He said that one of the local police departments had been involved in a major cover up a few years earlier regarding child pornography. Several officers were caught with it and were quickly and quietly dismissed. Bill wondered—since Rob admitted that he had been involved in child pornography, and since Rob revealed that he had a brother who worked as a police officer in one of the local police departments—if these incidents were somehow connected? And I wondered where Bill was getting all of this information. Would any of this new information help us in any way as far as That Group went? I didn't know; however, I did know that the deeper I dug, the stranger I found this dark world to be. No one could possibly make this stuff up!

Lastly I called Detective Charles. He said right away that he had not had a chance to call the other police department, and he was flabbergasted to learn that Rob had a brother in the other department! He relayed that he had tried to call Rob, but Rob had not answered. Detective Charles assured me that he would keep trying and that he would call the other police department soon. I hoped he would talk to Rob before Rob got cold feet. I hoped that Detective Charles would get going, period! I couldn't help but wonder if he ever got anything done! Some detective!

I think that Dr. Martin knows more about That Group than he lets on. What is he hiding from me? He did admit that he knew about the bruise on little Rory's face, but he tried to minimize it by saying it could have happened accidentally. He said he knows about all of the children standing in corners for hours at a time, but explained to me that he did not classify that as abuse.

I wondered what he was a doctor of, and where he had obtained his degree. How could he be so blind? What was he afraid of? Had he caught a glimpse of the Dark Ones? Were they as terrible as the ones I saw in my dreams? I wondered what the *real* connection was between Dr. Martin and That Group.

Some things are simply not what they first appear to be!

FEBRUARY 8, 1999

Early in the morning I called Carrie to let her know about what had been happening with Rob and Dr. Martin. She was encouraged by the new information. After I spoke with Carrie, I called Detective Charles, and what a nice surprise I got from him! He told me that he had spoken with Rob and that Rob was very forthcoming. Detective Charles stated that Rob was very talkative about the dark side of The Group. Detective Charles also said he believed Rob told him all that he knew, and that he was ready to cooperate fully with the police.

He also said he believed that Rob was fully committed to doing whatever needed to be done to bring That Group down. On top of all that, Detective Charles told me he had recorded all that Rob had said on a cassette player. Finally! Firsthand information! *Thank You, God!*

Detective Charles told me that Rob confessed that he had seen children stand facing walls for hours at a time as punishments for their sins. Also, Rob reiterated that the members of That Group hurled death threats and curses against the extended family members of those who belonged to That Group. Rob also confessed to the detective that he had seen Ray hit Rory and then throw Rory from his little chair and stomp on him. Stomp on him? What a monster Ray is! What monsters all of them are for watching such abuse and not reporting that abuse to the authorities! There is only darkness for these children, and in the darkness, the children hear the Dark Ones prowling about them! I am just repulsed!

But as repulsed as I feel, I felt even more repulsed when, at the end of my conversation with Detective Charles, he said to me that the statute of limitations *may* have run out for Ray's assault on little Rory, as well as other alleged atrocities. How could this be? How could Ray and the others get away with such violent behavior against the children?

FEBRUARY, 1999

I called Carrie. She has nothing new to report. She said she has called Detective Charles repeatedly and has not been successful in talking with him; he is always out of his office. She is very frustrated, and so am I! After I spoke with Carrie, I called Liz. She knew nothing new either. She did report that the court date for the boys had been set.

I then called Detective Charles. He apologized for the delay, and said he had not had a chance to follow up with Rob's confession and that he would work on it. What is wrong with him? Doesn't he care about the children? Why is he holding back? Why is he stalling? Why? What is going on?

I also spoke with Bill. He told me that a policeman had conversed with him and said that the statute of limitations on the battery charge against little Rory would run out soon.

What is wrong with all these people? Why aren't they going forward? Is one of the police departments protecting someone for some reason? Will they do nothing to help the children? Something is so wrong. Are they all merciless? Incompetent? *God have mercy!*

But where is God? I still have not found Him in any of my worlds except perhaps, in my dreams, in the garden. I thought I felt His presence in the garden the last time I dreamed I was there. I want to go back to the garden again! Soon! I need to search for God there—soon! I need some answers! I must find God!

Chapter 11

FEBRUARY 24, 1999

I had lunch with a woman, Gerrie, today during a Christian women's retreat. I had never met her before this. Imagine my surprise when I found out that we had something rather startling in common; she had, at one time, visited the little church where Annie and Bret got married—(the church from which That Group split off). She told me some very interesting facts about an experience she had at that little church. Gerrie said she had a sister who had been a member of that church, and that her sister had become concerned about some bizarre happenings going on there. Gerrie decided to visit the church, and she'd had an experience that was terrifying!

I asked her to explain. What she told me was the most bizarre story I had ever heard.

She explained that while visiting and participating in the worship service, she began to feel more and more uncomfortable—so uncomfortable that she did not want to participate in the service, but felt she had to stay because of her sister. So she stayed. About midway through the service, someone approached her and asked if she would please help in "catching" one or more of the young girls as they "fell backwards" during their "slaying of the spirit" rituals. Gerrie did not want to help, but she did not want to make a scene either. So she said she would help. Then, when she caught one of the girls falling backwards, she felt a huge jolt and found herself flying through the air. When she fell to the floor, she fell hard, and bruises began to bloom all over her body. Gerrie was very afraid, and when she returned home, she went to see her own pastor and told him about the incident and showed him some of her bruises. As it turned out, not only did she have bruises on her body, she also had scratch marks around each bruise. Her pastor told her she should tell the pastor of that little church about those bruises, so she did. That pastor, in turn, told her to go talk with a woman by the name of Jeze, so she did. When Gerrie spoke with Jeze, she was given a message from the girl that Gerrie had caught that night during the "slaying of the spirit" ritual. Jeze told her that the girl's message was this: "You are my prey. I will devour you."

Then Gerrie told me one more thing that happened during that service she had attended at that little church. She told me that Jeze had rolled her eyes at her and had growled at her like an animal. Gerrie and her sister have never returned to that church.

How strange that Gerrie and I met at that Christian women's retreat and discovered that our lives were somehow connected through very strange people and through some even stranger events.

After we talked, I asked if she might consider going to see Grayson or Bill and tell one or both of them what had happened to her. She said she would, and she did, and said Bill was amazed at all she told him. She also mentioned that Bill had received a nasty letter from a lawyer for That Group stating Bill had been very rude to call the police over the "boy in the hall" incident. Bill told her that the letter was extremely hateful.

A few days after I met Gerrie, I visited with Liz. She told me that the two boys would be going to court the following week and would go before Judge Day. Liz also mentioned she had spoken with Leah again, and that Leah had told her that her son, Stan, his wife Shelley, and their boys owned nothing! They had given all they had to That Group! Leah also said she gave the police a copy of her daughter-in-law's diary, which is filled with information about That Group.

FEBRUARY 25, 1999

I spoke with Liz again. She relayed information to me about the two boys. They had their day in court, and they will be sentenced next month. The court ordered the boys and their parents to have counseling. Home visits will be made by DCFS to the boys' home.

Liz also said that Stan and Shelley have attached "noise makers" to the boys' rooms so they can keep track of all their comings and goings in and out of their rooms. And also, Stan and Shelley have been frantically trying to clean up their home before the DCFS caseworker's visit.

MARCH 1, 1999

I called Detective Charles. He told me that things were moving forward. I really want to believe him.

MARCH 10, 1999

I am so tired . . .

MARCH 25, 1999

Leah called me yesterday. She was hysterical. She believes that her son, Stan, will kill her if she talks to the police about That Group or about their personal lives. She is genuinely frightened. I am frightened for her also!

Also today I made an appointment to see the top man of DCFS in our state, a Mr. Crum. We are set up to meet next week.

APRIL 3, 1999

Al and I traveled two hours to visit with Mr. Crum in his office. I was extremely nervous when we arrived. I wasn't sure if he would believe our story. My mind went foggy, and bile began climbing from my stomach to my throat. I took a seat and clasped my hands together for strength. I did not know where to start, and I felt so tongue-tied I wasn't sure if I could begin!

Mr. Crum was quite welcoming and gracious, yet I feared him. I feared that he would listen politely and then dismiss us thinking we were two people who had gone off the deep end. And even though I was sitting in his office, a part of me felt very far away; I could not seem to get myself together. I was thankful that Al was with me and could speak for us both.

We sat with him for about 90 minutes. As each minute passed, I began to gain some confidence. I began to feel less tongue-tied. He listened, he asked lots of questions, and he booted up his computer to see what he might find about the individuals involved in That Group. Unfortunately, he found very little. Apparently they had all been able to keep under the radar, even though the police and DCFS had been called in to investigate. He did ask quite a few questions about Rob. Interestingly, he said he had family ties in the Twin Cities where all of this was unfolding!

Al and I were able to give him quite a bit of information in the 90-minute timeframe offered to us, and he seemed truly amazed that we had acquired so many facts. When we were finished, Mr. Crum said that he was interested in our story and would contact Detective Charles, Rob, and the local DCFS, and then get back to us in a week or two.

It turned out to be a good visit, yet I did not leave feeling hopeful. I wondered to myself if Mr. Crum would indeed help us. Was he for real? I put on a hopeful face for my husband on the way home and settled my mind for a long wait—a wait of at least two weeks. There was nothing else I could do. I had no control over the situation—none at all.

APRIL 5, 1999

I had a vivid dream about Annie last night. She had just given birth to a baby girl. She allowed me to take the child for a while—for the day. I lovingly took care of the baby. I held her close. Then, at the end of the day, I brought her back to her mother. Annie was happy to see her child and me, together. I had bought some things for the baby and brought them with me. Annie was grateful. It was all so real. I felt so much love for my daughter and her baby. I so hated the fact that when I woke up, I realized it was all just a dream.

APRIL 6, 1999

There was a loud popping noise that came from my reading lamp during the evening, followed by a bright flash of light and an extremely loud, thunder-like noise. I thought the light bulb had exploded. I looked, but it had not. Very strange!

APRIL 22, 1999

The strange twists and turns in my life seem to continue. I found out that Ms. S., a member of That Group, and Rob's ex-wife, had the same name (maiden name) as Mr. Crum, the top DCFS man of in our state! I wondered if she was related to Mr. Crum! That might explain why Mr. Crum asked so many questions about Rob and why he had not yet gotten back to me. Mr. Crum did tell me that his mother lived in the Twin Cities. There couldn't be that many people in the Twin Cities with that last name!

I called Carrie and told her about the name coincidence. She told me she would try to find out if there might be a relationship. Then Carrie gave me some up-to-date information about Leah's extended family. Apparently, the boys got off with probation and went home. Now Stan is furious with Leah and John and is blaming all of his boys' problems on them. And Stan has cut off relationships with his parents for the second time! He wants to go back to That Group! He is saving whatever dollars he can so that he can buy his way back in. In the meantime, Stan is trying to get whatever he can out of his parents. But John and Leah won't have it and are trying to get everything they have given to their son and his family back, including the carpet right off the floor and the telephones!

Where are You God? Why do You let this situation continue? Have You abandoned all of us? Why don't You come to save us from all of this? Where are You hiding?

APRIL 25, 1999

I am at a very low point, and I feel extremely fragile. Mr. Crum has not yet called back. He has not answered a single message that I have left for him.

No one ever seems to get back with me in a timely manner; no one seems to want to help. I don't know where else to go for help. I seem to be at a dead end. In the meantime, the statute of limitations regarding the assault of little Rory has probably run out. Hope is also running out.

I dreamed of Annie and Bret and the children last night. In my dream, I was in their home. Things were tense but not terrible. The children were happy to see me. But then I woke up. It was just another dream: Nothing was real, nothing had changed . . . nothing at all.

It's already August of 1999. I spoke with Leah last week. She told me that a woman named Sue wanted to speak with me. Sue's step-grandchild, Tim, has recently come out of That Group, and apparently he is "messed up." Neither Leah nor I were sure what that meant. Tim's mother was still a member of That Group and is not happy that her son left. Apparently she told her son to get out of her house. According to Leah, Tim is now living with a friend.

I also spoke with Liz last week. She has seen her children and grandchildren again (by camping out in the parking lot of the mall that houses That Group's space). She relayed to me that Ray's youngest daughter has dark blonde hair, and that Bret's little girl has light blonde hair. She said they were both beautiful. Liz believes that both Theresa and Annie are pregnant again!

In September I decided to talk to Carrie again. I had not spoken with her for a while. I asked her if she had been able to get any information about the "the Crum family." She told me she had not. She did tell me, however, that her granddaughter, Cassie, has been in the "spotlight" inside That Group lately, because the members had deemed her as "Evil." (Cassie's older brother, Paulie, had informed Carrie of this situation in a very matter-of-fact way.)

I can only imagine what terror Cassie might be experiencing—what punishments she may be enduring—at the hands of the leaders. I so wish that Carrie would intervene somehow. Her husband is a lawyer for heaven's sakes! Is she afraid that her son, Tom, will take the children away from her if she tells her story to the Police or to DCFS? Is she afraid that if she intervenes, little Paulie will get in trouble for telling, and that the punishments might get worse for Cassie? I do understand that Carrie and her husband are in a difficult situation. They do not want to lose their visitation rights, but do they ever think of what all of the other children are enduring?

My sister Patty, called me. She told me she had sent Annie a birthday card and that the card had come back from the post office with a new address written on it. Annie and Bret have moved! I need to call Liz and Carrie and tell them about the move. The three of us need to check out the address that was stamped on Patty's returned envelope.

There is too much going on in my head. Everything is swirling around. The wheels on the bus are spinning and spinning—but the bus is not going anywhere. I am weary of trying to be normal; I am weary of the nightmares. I am weary of the glimpses I have had into the dark world my daughter lives in. I am weary of it all!

The beautiful garden seems to be the only place where my soul can rest. I hope I will see God the next time I go there.

Chapter 12

In late October, 1999, Carrie called me with some news. She told me Cassie and Paulie were with their other set of grandparents last weekend and the children spilled lots of information to them about That Group. The children told their grandparents the following:

"Ray scares us when he preaches. He shouts and yells and uses the "S" word. He also uses the "D" word and the "F" word when he gets worked up. He touches his privates when he is talking to us. He hurts Rory when Rory does something bad. One time Ray picked him up and threw him across the room and then kneed him in the stomach and private parts, all because Rory had forgotten to tie his shoes and that made Ray mad. One time Ray got mad at a little girl and slapped her across the face. We are afraid of Ray."

I thanked Carrie for her news but I doubted that it would make any difference. Not unless the other set of grandparents were willing to go to the authorities!

There are many days when I wonder if I have gone completely mad. The new world I have created is filled with countless dead-ends, delays, unreturned calls, secondhand information, ears that will not listen, mouths that are silent, eyes that look away, and minds that do not understand. Sometimes I ask myself if I, like Alice, have fallen down a rabbit hole. Do I live in the pages of a book? Are my enemies a stack of cards? Will I wake from my new world just as someone cries out to me, "Off with her head!"

NOVEMBER 13, 1999

Kate and I went to see Detective Charles. As it turned out, he was unavailable, but we were able to speak with two other detectives. One of them told us that the entire situation had gotten to a new level. He gave Kate and me a report form to fill out, and we filed charges against Ray for aggravated battery against a child. We also mentioned the other children by name that were involved in That Group.

After we finished with the form, we were assigned a case number and told that our case was being transferred from the Intelligence Unit to the Crime Unit. Then we were told that a juvenile officer would be assigned to our case and that he would be working with Detective Charles.

Finally we were told that Detective Charles was working with DCFS and that there would possibly be some surveillance done. We left the police department feeling some hope again that something might finally be done.

NOVEMBER 16, 1999

I spoke with Carrie. She told me that Detective Charles called her and would like for Cassie and Paulie to come in for questioning. Carrie is a wreck. She is afraid that if the children go in for questioning, she will lose all visitation rights.

NOVEMBER 27, 1999

Kate called one of the detectives at the police department. He told Kate that he and Detective Charles would be going over the case today. He also told Kate that he had set up a meeting between little Paulie and the Advocacy Center, but Carrie had intervened and put a stop to it.

Here we were again! Not sure if we are going to move forward. I am so discouraged. So sad. Hope has all but vanished, and all seems lost. All we can do is just keep putting one foot in front of the other and try to survive . . .

Bill called. He had just had an unpleasant encounter with Jeze. Apparently he had parked in one of the parking spaces That Group claimed as their own. They came out of the building and shouted at him, telling him that he was not a Christian. They told him that he was violating the law of God and that he would be judged! Then Jeze began to verbally attack him using

Scripture, and she mocked him as she swayed back and forth. Her eyes were filled with hatred!

The Dark Ones are everywhere! They want to destroy our souls. They are filled with hate and with murderous thoughts. Are there any heroes left—anywhere? Heroes who are willing to fight the Dark Angels? I know You are out there somewhere, God! Please send Your Army of Angels! Please show Your face! Surely Your Presence is somewhere in this place!

Everything ended up going south in the Fall of 1999. Nothing turned out the way I had hoped: the statute of limitations ran out, the police department ceased to contact us, DCFS ceased to contact us, families of those who had children and grandchildren involved in That Group drifted apart, the defectors from That Group remained silent, and even my lawyer was silent. It seemed as if there was nothing more that could be done. No one seemed interested in helping us or in going forward at all. Not even God. It was finished. The Prince of Darkness and his Dark Angels had won. My life was broken into a million pieces.

Humpty Dumpty sat on a wall.
Humpty Dumpty had a great fall.
And all the king's horses,
And all the king's men,
Couldn't put Humpty together again.
—A children's nursery rhyme

All the king's horses and all the king's men couldn't put Humpty together again. No one could. Humpty would never be whole again. And neither would I.

PART 3

Do not be afraid, but go on speaking and do not be silent, for I am with you, and no one will harm you or attack you, for I have many in this city who are my people (Acts 18: 9-10).

Chapter 13

In the children's fairy tale, "The Emperor's New Clothes," the Emperor and his subjects were blind as bats the day he paraded up and down the street in his brand new "clothes." But in fact, the Emperor was not dressed at all! He was parading around naked! The adults did not want to see what really was, and so they did not. They all pretended that he was dressed, until a small child spoke up and exclaimed, "The Emperor has no clothes!" And at once they all saw the truth—the Emperor was indeed naked!

How foolish we all are from time to time! Even in fairy tales. How God can love His foolish people is beyond my understanding!

Jesus knew how foolish His people could be. In John 8:37-46, He said this to His people: "I know that you are Abraham's descendants. Yet you are looking for a way to kill me, because you have no room for my word. I am telling you what I have seen in the Father's presence, and you are doing what you have heard from your father."

"Abraham is our father," they answered.

"If you were Abraham's children," said Jesus, "then you would do what Abraham did. As it is, you are looking for a way to kill me, a man who has told you the truth that I heard from God. Abraham did not do such things. You are doing the works of your own father."

"We are not illegitimate children," they protested. "The only Father we have is God Himself."

Jesus said to them, "If God were your Father, you would love Me, for I have come here from God. I have not come on My own; God sent Me. Why is My language not clear to you? Because you are unable to hear what I say. You belong to your father, the devil, and you want to carry out your father's desires. He was a murderer from the beginning, not holding to the truth, for there is no truth in him. When he lies, he speaks in his native language, for he is a liar and the father of lies. Yet because I tell the truth, you do not believe Me! Can any of you prove Me guilty of sin? If I am telling the truth, why don't you believe Me?"

How foolish we all are from time to time. How God can love His foolish people is beyond my understanding!

Little Miss Muffet
Sat on a tuffet,
Eating her curds and whey.
Then along came a spider
And sat down beside her
Scaring Miss Muffet away.
—A children's nursery rhyme

This is such an innocent sounding nursery rhyme about a little girl being just that—a little girl—and doing what a little girl might do—having a tea party with her dolls and her teddy bears—and not paying a bit of attention to a small spider that is about to enter her world. Such a small thing—that spider—but it comes to her tea party and scares her. And she runs away, taking matters into her own hands, knowing that her mother might tell her that spiders are not scary at all. The little girl knows that her Mama does not always tell her the truth. She knows that her Mama likes to pretend. Children are often far more perceptive than their grownups think they are. Many children know that their grownups like to live in fairy tales that end only with happily ever afters.

How foolish we all are from time to time, even in fairy tales. How God can love His foolish people is beyond my understanding.

> *Three blind mice.*
> *Three blind mice.*
> *See how they run.*
> *See how they run.*
> *They all ran after the farmer's wife,*
> *Who cut off their tails with a carving*
> *knife.*
> *Have you ever seen such a sight in your*
> *life.*
> *As three blind mice.*
> *—A child's nursery rhyme*

Sometimes grownups run blindly away from truths they don't want to hear and instead follow whoever or whatever they want to follow as long as whatever they are running after lines up with what they believe to be true. And sometimes grownups end up in pieces, like the three blind mice.

How foolish we all are from time to time, even in fairy tales. How God can love His foolish people is beyond my understanding!

Long ago I was fooled by the Father of Lies and his army of Dark Ones. I didn't want to see them. I didn't want to hear them. I didn't want to know the truth. And when I finally recognized them, it was too late. My life broke into pieces. My daughter's life broke into pieces. My grandchildren's lives broke into pieces. How foolish I was.

And every night I pray for them:

> *Now I lay them down to sleep,*
> *I pray thee Lord their souls to keep.*
> *And if they die before they wake*
> *I pray thee Lord their souls to take.*

And every night and every day I am haunted by my grandchildren's voices:

"Help us, Grandma! Tell someone what happened to us. Maybe someone will believe you. Maybe someone will come for us! Don't give up, Grandma! Never give up! Don't quit until you are done "

And somewhere in the midst of those young voices I think I hear an older one:

"I am so sorry. I have to stay. I have to take care of the children. Forgive me. I love you. Don't give up! Don't quit until you are done!"

But I don't know how to help them. How foolish I was. How foolish . . . how foolish . . . how foolish. My life is in pieces, and I don't know what to do.

Chapter 14

I had so wanted to help my grandchildren after the fall of 1999. I had so wanted to sweep the spiders and all the other scary things out of their lives. But I did not know how.

Very little happened for a year or so after that Fall when the police investigation had come to an abrupt halt. The children's souls had screamed out that Fall, but the police were unable to move forward. The children's souls had screamed out that Fall, but social services was not able to move forward. The children's souls had screamed out that Fall, but the people who left That Group did nothing for fear that their lives were in danger. The children's souls had screamed out at *me* that Fall, but I had been weak and did not do enough to help them. Today the children's souls *still* cry out for help, and still—no one seems to be able to help them.

Al and I were totally crushed, disillusioned, and

battle-weary after the Fall of 1999. No one knew how to help the children. And my husband and I felt like complete failures as parents and as grandparents. It was then that Al and I decided to take a deep breath and make some changes. We could no longer continue our lives as is. The new world we had built was not working, at least for now. And we felt we could no longer do anything for Annie, Bret, and our grandchildren. Thus, in late 2000, we accepted new jobs in a new location, hoping we could escape from some of the pain and weariness of the battle—at least for a little while. And for a time, we did feel some relief, as our energy was diverted into thinking about new beginnings, it seemed as if our souls, what was left of them, took refuge in being busy.

The past began to fade a bit around the edges. The children's voices became whispers. The one lone adult voice I thought I heard was no more. And we slowly began to accept the fact that our middle daughter was gone. Her husband and children were gone. And nothing more could be done—unless God Himself rescued them . . . and we couldn't find God anywhere.

A little over a year after I thought we were done with the battle, done with the Darkness and done with the Dark Ones and just as we were getting ready to move into a new state and a new home and new jobs, I received a copy of a letter from my daughter and her husband, via my lawyer, Rudy, who had been in contact with them about our move. The letter was brief, and it was cruel. It stated that Al and I would never be allowed to trespass on their property or leave gifts or goods of any kind on their property—neither would any agent or friend of mine. Further, I would never be allowed to contact any of their family at any time. Nor would any of my agents or friends ever be allowed to make contact with them.

Darkness had raised its ugly head again; the Dark Ones wanted more of our souls. The battle was not over! We could not ignore that letter! Strangely, even though the letter had come from my daughter, the letter did not seem to be written *by* my daughter. For even though my daughter had signed the letter, it seemed to have been written by a stranger. The letter used words and phrases that she had never used before. The words were stiff, cold, and cruel. Perhaps it was the Dark Angel who had written the words.

That letter made me realize I could not just sit back and do nothing; I had rested enough. I could not let the Darkness win. Al and I would never be able to escape from the Dark Angels holding my daughter, my son-in-law, and my grandchildren as hostages if we did nothing. And I could no longer muffle the sounds of my grandchildren's voices crying out in the night without answering them!

But at the same time, I simply did not know what

to do. I did not know where to start. And so Al and I prayed. And we waited for God's wisdom. But we heard nothing from God. Lord God, the battle of good and evil rages within and around us, and our ancient foe tempts us with his deceits and empty promises. Keep us steadfast in Your Word, and, when we fall, raise us again and restore us!

My daughter still wanted *nothing more* to do with me—with any of us. Nothing had changed, nothing at all. Had the Dark Ones made their final kill? Had their souls been completely obliterated? Had the Dark Angel cast an unbreakable curse on Annie?

> *My God, my God, why have you*
> *abandoned us?*
> *Why are you so far away?*
> *Won't you listen to our groans and come*
> *to our rescue?*
> *I cry out day and night, but you don't*
> *answer.*
> *I can never rest.*
> *—Psalm 22:1-2*

Chapter 15

EARLY 2002

Last night I had a vivid dream of Annie and her family. I continue to have dreams of her from time to time, but they have been rare. In the dream, Annie seemed happy to see me—but was tired, depressed, and lethargic. There was no real life within her at all. Someone, or something, had stolen her soul. She appeared to be soul-less.

In my dream, Bret was nearby. He was also depressed, as were their children. One little girl needed her diaper changed, but no one had enough energy to change it. The little girl did not fuss. Perhaps she was used to wearing soiled diapers. The only life I saw came from their youngest child, a baby boy who appeared to be 10-12 months old. He was happily walking around and getting into everything. He exuded life compared to the others, and he seemed to be oblivious to all the lifelessness around him. He knew that his mother loved him, despite her lack of attention, and that seemed enough for him. The little boy had bright red hair that stood out clearly in the midst of the darkness and lethargy all around.

Perhaps that red hair was a sign of hope—a light in the darkness.

AUGUST, 2002

I received a newspaper clipping from my sister stating that the governor of our state had signed a new law allowing grandparents to sue for visitation rights with their estranged grandchildren. Feeling a bit of new hope, I called my lawyer, but Rudy gave me a word of caution. He told me that the new law would not go into effect until January 2003. He also told me that we would have to go for a "mental incompetency" investigation for Annie and Bret. His words hit me hard. Did things need to be this difficult? After all, I still loved my daughter and her family. How could we do this without hurting them?

SEPTEMBER, 2002

The nightmares have begun again. Last night I had a dream about rats—big ugly rats. They were everywhere in my house. Everywhere! I tried to pretend that they were not there—but they were there! They would not go away! I tried to kill them, but they would not die! I was terrified!

SEPTEMBER, 2002

Tomorrow I will go to see my lawyer, Rudy. I have no clue how that meeting will go. I have sent him over 100 typed pages of information from my journals.

LATE SEPTEMBER, 2002

I met with my lawyer and he asked me to provide more information about my daughter and her family. He wanted social security numbers, a home phone number, Bret's work number, and their address. He wanted a description of their physical characteristics. He then said that the only way to go forward would be to try to find Annie and Bret incompetent, and added that it would be a long shot—a very expensive long shot. He did not seem very hopeful; neither did I. He did say that he would like to hire a private investigator for the case if I wanted to pursue one. Well, perhaps there was a bit of hope in that.

OCTOBER, 2002

My lawyer called. He has hired a private investigator by the name of Ted. (This is the third or fourth time this name has come up!) My lawyer needs a check to send to him for $1,500.00 to get started on the case. I sent him the check.

LATE OCTOBER, 2002

Ted called me today. He asked lots of questions. I told him I would send him a copy of my journals, along with copies of letters from my daughter, a copy of the police report I had filled out, and the "witness list" I told him I could put together. I also gave him a few names of people he could contact who had some information that might be useful.

I am trying to stay calm, but it's almost impossible.

I can't sleep at night. I am tired and nauseated most of the time. I don't even know how to pray. What exactly should I pray for? My hopes are high, but I worry that they will soon be dashed—again—and that there will be nothing anyone can do—again. I am in the middle of a war and I don't know what to do!

From Revelation 12:

> *Then war broke out in heaven. Michael and his angels fought against the dragon, and the dragon and his angels fought back. But the dragon was not strong enough, and they lost their place in heaven. The great dragon was hurled down, that ancient serpent called the devil, or Satan, who leads the whole world astray. He was hurled to earth, and his angels with him. Lord God help us to hurl the dragon out of our lives!*

OCTOBER 20, 2002

I heard from Ted today via email. He has read through the entire journal and he plans to read it again "more slowly." He said he would get back to me.

OCTOBER 22, 2002

Sarah to Ted via email:

> I was so happy to get your email! I am looking forward to talking with you in the morning! I did speak with Liz this past week. She said she would be willing to speak with you. But she is very

fragile, as are all of us who have kids and grandkids in this Group. I believe that a woman named Carrie, and her husband, Jason, will also speak with you, as well as Grayson, our counselor, and his assistant, Bill. I think Detective Charles also wants to speak with you as well as a man named Rob. I don't know about anyone else right now. I have not spoken to them for at least 18 months—except for Liz. Talk to you in the morning.

OCTOBER 23, 2002

Ted called me this morning and we talked for about 2 hours. He asked me lots of questions about the journals. He said he has already done some background checks on some of the main characters in my story and found out that both Bret and Ray have been involved with drugs over the years. Ted is also very interested in Rob. He said he also wants to speak with Detective Charles and any other people in that police department who may know about the case. He also wants to talk to the landlord at the mall where all of these strange meetings are taking place. There's one more thing—Ted told me that this is the strangest case he has ever worked on!

OCTOBER 28, 2002

I received a letter from Rudy today. He is furious with me for showing Ted a copy of my journals! What is up with that? Rudy is the one who suggested hiring Ted to head up the investigation!

OCTOBER 29, 2002

Ted to Sarah via email:

If you don't mind my asking, what did your lawyer say in his letter? He doesn't know me very well and may have thought I was complaining about the amount of documents you sent to me. I know I commented to him that you sent me more papers than you first indicated you would. I also commented to him about reading some of your disturbing dreams. But I wasn't complaining and I found the materials very informative and very much worth the time it took me to read everything. It gave me some helpful background information on the case and on some of the people involved. Maybe you should tell Rudy that we might plan to meet with certain people. I want you to do whatever you're comfortable with, but I will tell you that I think a meeting would be extremely helpful to my investigation. You might tell Rudy that he can call me if he wishes to. Also, I think there is a chance that Carrie and her husband might not want to get directly involved in the investigation, for fear it would affect their visitation rights with their grandchildren. However, if they could at least tell me what they know regarding this Group, it would be helpful. I will contact them next.

NOVEMBER 1, 2002

Sarah to Ted via email:

Thank you for your last email. I can't understand what the fuss is all about over my journals. I have been writing these journals for years! I did not prepare them specifically for Rudy. I just don't know why I have to keep it all a secret from you!

NOVEMBER 2, 2002

Ted to Sarah via email:

I will call you later this morning.

NOVEMBER 3, 2002

Ted to Sarah via email:

Sorry I was unable to call you the end of last week. My wife and I had an emergency situation with one of our pets. We had to rush one of our cats to the University Small Animal Clinic yesterday morning. Prior to heading to the hospital I did speak on the telephone with Carrie, and she is willing to meet with you and I and anyone else you can round up. I need to go to my office and check my calendar and then get back with you about some possible dates to meet.

NOVEMBER 4, 2002

Sarah to Ted via email:

I am so sorry that your cat is ill. I am an animal lover too. I have a 12-year-old dog and a 5-year-old cat. Before we had these pets we had two cats for 18 years. I spoke with Liz today and she is willing to meet with us this Friday or next Friday. See if that matches up with any free time on your schedule and call me or email when you get a chance.

NOVEMBER 5, 2002

Ted to Sarah via email:

This coming Friday may work. Unfortunately we had to put our cat down this morning. We tried everything to save her, but she had too many organs involved with some type of problem and we didn't want her to suffer anymore. I will call you tomorrow morning.

NOVEMBER 6, 2002

Sarah to Ted via email:

So sorry to hear about your cat. We had to put our two cats down a few years ago. It was devastating for our family. Looking forward to talking with you tomorrow.

NOVEMBER 7, 2002

Ted called, and we decided to meet on Friday. During our conversation, one of the things he told me was that he had tried to contact one of the detectives from the local police department. However, it seems that this particular detective has retired and knows nothing about the case! How convenient! Our case had been reassigned to this detective at one point in time. There must be a paper trail somewhere, but maybe not—nothing surprises me anymore. Many people don't do what they are supposed to do: things disappear, people lie, or they forget things on purpose—even good people—even police departments. Yes, sometimes the Dark Ones inhabit police departments.

NOVEMBER 7, 2002, EVENING

Sarah to Ted via email: I felt very down after our conversation this morning. How could we have run into a dead end in that police department? This stuff did not happen that long ago! Sometimes I just don't know if we will ever make any headway. My soul is heavy. Did you get my phone message about meeting on Friday? I called shortly after our early morning conversation. Both Liz and Carrie can meet with us this Friday for sure. I wish all of this wasn't so difficult. I will have to make a 9-hour trip on Thursday, stay overnight with my sister, and then meet with all of you on Friday before driving another 9 hours back home! I am so unsure of where all of this is going. Maybe nowhere. Maybe I will just have to accept the fact that I may never see my beautiful daughter's face again. My soul is so weary. I am sending you the names of all of the adults that I believe are still involved with this Group. I know of only 12 adults involved at this time and about 10-12 children. The group has definitely diminished in size. Their High Priestess, Jezebelle, has taken all of their souls. Some days I feel like she has taken mine, too.

I lift my eyes to the hills
From where is my help to come?
My help comes from the Lord,
The maker of heaven and earth.
The Lord will not let my foot be moved
Nor will the one who watches over me
fall asleep.
Behold, the keeper of Israel
Will neither slumber nor sleep;
The Lord watches over me;
The Lord is my shade at my right hand;
The sun will not strike me by day
Nor the moon by night.
The Lord will preserve me from all evil
And will keep my life.
The Lord will watch over my going out
and my coming in,
From this time forth
For evermore.
—Psalm 121

Heal me, Lord! Make me strong—strong enough to fight. I want the faith that the writer of this Psalm had. I want to believe what he wrote.

NOVEMBER 8, 2002

Ted to Sarah via email:

Don't give up hope, and please try to be patient. I know it's difficult. But, I won't ever lie to you and say that I think finding the right piece of this puzzle will be easy. We just need to keep exploring our options. I think that we will have a better idea of what we're faced with after this meeting on Friday. It sounds as if this Group has tightened its circle. Most likely, some of your prior attempts to find a solution to this problem (I'm mainly referring to the police report and the DCFS complaint) have gotten back to the members of this Group and may have caused them to stop some of the abuse. Lack of this type of abuse is good for the children, but is rather bad from an investigative standpoint. I need to know more about this Grandparent Law that is coming into effect after the first of the year. It may help guide me in what exactly will help your situation the most. Anyway, I just want you to keep an open mind until we can see what is out there.

NOVEMBER 9, 2002

Sarah to Ted via email:

Thank you for your note of encouragement. If nothing else, maybe I have prevented those children from being abused these past couple of years, at least physically. I know that is no small thing. So perhaps my efforts thus far have helped the children after all. I will bring you a copy of the law that Rudy sent me. It is very lengthy. I haven't read it all. Besides that, I can't even begin to understand all of the legal jargon. You have already found some information about this Group and that it exists. Sometimes I feel I have lost touch with reality and that somewhere in my mind I have made it all up. It is all so bizarre. The fact that you have found some information on this Group and that there is a Jeze helps me to see that it is indeed real and I have not gone completely and utterly mad! I do know this—if you find something on any of them that will make their lives uncomfortable, they will be very angry! If they find out that I am at the bottom of it and that you were hired to find out about them, they may come after us!

NOVEMBER 9, 2002

Ted to Sarah via email:

I will meet you at Bob Evans at 9:00a.m. on Friday.

FRIDAY—THE DAY OF OUR APPOINTED MEETING

I met with Ted for about an hour before we met with Liz and Carrie. He is a very nice man, and I can tell that he is very smart. I think I can trust him. Ted is also very gracious and easy to talk to. He asked me lots of questions. I did not know what to expect when Ted, Liz, Carrie, and I all met together, but amazingly, both Carrie and Liz were welcoming and full of information to share. I felt so grateful. I didn't have to say much of anything; everything they told Ted I had already written about in my journals. (It was proof that I had not lost my mind! Everything I had written was true.) I believe that Ted really wants to help us. I don't know if he can, but I know that he wants to.

I did find out a few new facts today. Ray is no longer the group's lead preacher. He has been "dethroned" and is just a "regular person" now. Jeze and her daughter have taken central stage at all of the meetings. Also, a woman by the name of Julia is no longer a "Princess" and she no longer has any special powers. Perhaps this group is beginning to crumble.

Ted took lots of notes at our meeting. He said he would talk to Rudy next week. I am thankful for that. I am so glad that we had this meeting!

LATE NOVEMBER, 2002

Ted to Sarah via email:

> It was great to finally meet you last Friday. I hope you had a good drive home. Though we didn't develop a lot of

new information, I was pleased to hear that Jeze may be trying to take more control over this Group. I would hope this move, on her part, would mean the Group might be collapsing. When we met, you mentioned that the children in this Group were being homeschooled and you wondered what kinds of regulations our state has on homeschooling. I spoke with a lady here in town that has had a long career as a school superintendent. She said that homeschooling is not regulated or overseen by the school system, or anyone else in our state! There seems to be no qualifying standards, laws, or regulations regarding this kind of schooling. The schools do not approve the curriculum, and the testing of the children/ students is not standardized. There are no qualification requirements for the teachers. It really amazes me! Apparently people conducting homeschooling may register with the school districts, but it is not required. There are homeschooling packets available, but again, there is no requirement that they be obtained. Also, I have been curious as to how this religious group maintains itself financially. I contacted a friend of mine who is a CPA and asked him about churches, or religious organizations, that have a not-for-profit status. He said that, to his knowledge, these types of entities don't have to file anything because the funds they take in are considered donations and are not taxable. I will be making some phone calls in the coming week to some of the people on the list you gave me (those who were former members of this Group). I hope they will cooperate. Perhaps we can talk by telephone sometime yet this week and discuss our options.

Sarah to Ted via email:

Hi Ted. It was good to meet you too. Thanks for your email. I am dismayed and shocked that our state does not have any regulations regarding homeschooling. There may be quite a few children in our state who are not sent to school and who receive little to no education at home. Do these children even exist to their communities? Or are they living in the shadows? How will they function as adults? Who protects them? Hopefully they get regular medical care. But what if they don't? On another note, I would like to know why Detective Charles did nothing after my daughter, Kate, and I filed a complaint against Ray a couple of years ago. In fairness, maybe he did do something—but he never got back to me. Ray committed a felony against a child. Why wasn't he arrested? If he was, why wasn't I informed? Privacy laws perhaps?

Ted to Sarah via email:

My CPA friend called yesterday with a little more information on religious organizations and their not-for-profit status. It doesn't take much for these organizations to be exempt from paying taxes. However, he tells me that there is some record of the local religious organizations that are properly exempt and he is going to check on That Group your daughter is involved with. I suspect they are probably exempt because they have a member who is an accountant and because the corporation is shown to be not-for-profit. But it doesn't hurt to check it out.

Al to Ted via email:

Are there records to check to see if they are paying the employer portion of federal and state taxes and FICA for their paid employees? Just a thought.

Ted to Sarah via email:

I'm faxing a copy of an article that was in the November issue of the Illinois Bar Journal regarding the new law that's coming in on Grandparents' Visitation Rights. This article is much easier to understand than the article supplied to you by Rudy. I hope you find it interesting and helpful. It appears to me that this new law gives you more of a right to argue that the kids should be entitled to have a relationship with their grandparents. Please call me early next week so that we can discuss the investigation. Hope the two of you have a great Thanksgiving!

Sarah to Ted via email:

Thank you so much for the article you sent. It does seem way more helpful than the one that Rudy sent. It seems to me that we would not need to prove that Annie and Bret are unfit parents, only that it would be best for the children—mentally and emotionally—to have some contact with their grandparents and other extended family members. I feel cautiously optimistic that something might be able to be done for these children. I would feel even better if Rudy would feel optimistic enough to go ahead with the case or at least to continue with the investigation. Have a blessed Thanksgiving and I will call you next week.

Chapter 16

On Wednesday in early December, Ted and I spoke for about an hour on the phone. He said he had received quite a bit of new information from his conversations with Grayson and Evin. Ted also spoke to our lawyer, Rudy (who still wants to go with the "incompetency" route). Ted then asked a lawyer friend of his what he thought about the new Grandparents' Law, and if there might be another route besides claiming "incompetency" for Annie and Bret. Ted's lawyer friend told him that he thought there was something else we might be able to do.

Maybe I need a new lawyer. Lawyer number 3.

The next day, I spoke at length with Liz. She found out that five former members of That Group were attending a new church in town. Three of them, Katie K., David, and Leah, might be willing to talk to Ted about their experiences with That Group. The other two might be more reluctant. Liz told me that Katie K. was recently run out of That Group and might have the most up-to-date information.

In mid-December, Ted called me with a lot of fresh information from Evin—a whistle blower of heroic proportions! According to Evin:

Jeze's behavior is akin to those engaged in witchcraft.

Jeze's preachings are strange and non-scripturally based.

Liz and Dan were cut off from their children/grandchildren because they are Catholic!

Evin does not know why Sarah and Al were cut off.

Jeze wants control of everyone—including all of the children.

Jeze has always wanted her daughter to marry a "Strongman" who could be used as her "mouth piece."

Jeze gave her daughter's husband, Ray, more and more power and control, but he did not have the gifts Jeze hoped for.

Ray has a history of drug and alcohol addictions.

Ray's preaching is mainly made up of intimidation, yelling, and screaming.

Members are required to contribute large portions of their income to That Group.

Jeze's husband handles all of the group's finances.

A small salary is provided for the head pastor.

Ray threatens people with various kinds of fear tactics. He often points his finger right in a person's face.

Evin says that he knows of at least 4 kids who were physically abused—2 of them teenaged boys, 1 of whom spoke to Evin at length about the abuse. (Evin will not reveal the identity of these children.)

Be alert and sober of mind. Your enemy the devil prowls around like a roaring lion looking for someone to devour. Resist him, standing firm in the faith, because you know that the family of believers throughout the world is undergoing the same kind of sufferings (1 Peter 5:8-9).

Be careful, Ted! Watch your back. The owl with talons, razor sharp, may be after your soul also!

LATE DECEMBER, 2002

Ted to Sarah via email:

I wanted you to know that I have talked with two different attorneys about the procedure regarding Grandparents' Visitation Rights with their grandchildren. The first lawyer said he believes that you could merely file a petition and not have to prove that your daughter is incompetent. He said he would research the issue and get back with me. He seemed to indicate that you would be better off to get a lawyer closer to where your daughter lives. The second lawyer is in a neighboring office. He does a lot of family law cases. He also said that he thought you would not need to prove your daughter incompetent, but said the law is confusing and needs to be sorted out in the courts. He is willing to talk to you by telephone. Again you may need to get a new lawyer here where your daughter resides. But you will need to talk to your present lawyer about the situation. I don't want to go behind his back with anything. If I don't talk to you before then, I hope you and Al have a good Christmas.

DECEMBER 24, 2002

Ted to Sarah via email:

Two quick things: We may find out that your present lawyer is correct about needing to show your daughter and her husband somehow as incompetent parents. But even if this is right, you might want to consider getting a lawyer in the county where they live and where the petition would have to be filed. My second thought is that if you are able to file a petition, it might be helpful if Liz and Dan file a petition at the same time. This way it wouldn't look like just one side of the grandparents had been denied contact/visitation with these children, that in fact, both sets of grandparents have been denied contact. I don't know if Liz and her husband would want to do this, and maybe it isn't a good idea, but something to consider. I also think, if it would be allowed, that the petition(s) should indicate that not only have the grandparents been denied contact, but also Annie and Bret have severed contact with all of their respective siblings. I believe these types of facts would illustrate how weird and inappropriate Bret and Annie's behavior is.

DECEMBER 28, 2002

Ted called me today and went over everything he had written in his email. We spoke for quite a while. I don't know what I would do without Ted right now. Ted said he wants to talk to more people.

DECEMBER 29, 2002

Sarah to Ted via email:

It was good to talk to you yesterday. Right after you called, I called Liz. Then I called a woman named Leah and asked her if she would mind speaking with you. She told me that she is willing to help in any way she can. She also told me that her entire family has been hurt by That Group headed by Jeze. Actually, she said that Evin had, at one time, also been very cruel to her. I relayed to her that Evin is now out of the Group. Anyway, she had much to say and she hopes that Jeze will be brought down. She believes that her daughter and her husband will also speak with you. Everything she described to me lined up with my writings from my journals. I feel validated! Just when I think I am going crazy someone new validates me. I am thankful for that. Leah said she knows of others who may be willing to talk to you. There have been so many people who have been hurt by Jeze and her puppet followers and leaders. In the meantime, Ted, you are getting in deeper and deeper. The Dark Ones are closing in. The Prince of Darkness is furious! Be careful!

DECEMBER 29, 2002

Ted to Sarah via email:

I think you should probably wait to talk with Liz about also filing a petition until you talk with an attorney regarding my suggestion. A lawyer may not agree with this idea of mine, though I don't see that it could hurt anything. I guess the other thought is that the petitions most likely could not be filed jointly and the petitions could also end up being heard by different judges and then the effect of the petitions filed at the same time would be nil. I have a call in to my good friend Hazel and will let you know what she thinks. Have a good New Year. I'm hoping next year will be a great year for you and your family.

JANUARY, 2003

Ted to Sarah via email:

> I had not heard back from my friend Hazel until today when she left a message. She and I spoke briefly in person late this afternoon. What she said was not real encouraging, but she has offered to talk with you and tell you the step-by-step things that need to be done if you want to try to file a petition. I can brief her about the situation before you talk with her. On another note: Carrie called me yesterday. She had some new information, which I will share with you when we talk. I look forward to talking with you soon.

JANUARY 6, 2003

Ted called today with some new information from Carrie:

Her grandson, Paulie, has been enrolled in a military school. Apparently Paulie was having major behavioral problems in the public school he was attending. Carrie is very upset, as she will get to see Paulie even less.

Carrie asked Ted about the statute of limitations regarding child abuse. She stated that, about a year ago, one of the little girls (about 5 years old) in the group was punished severely after committing some kind of minor infraction. Carrie believes she merely lifted up her skirt. This little girl was made to stand in front of the group's members while they taunted her and made fun of her. The little girl began to sob; and tears and snot began to roll down her cheeks onto the floor. Then they made her lick it all up.

Carrie also explained that Paulie was punished for a small infraction in the same horrible way. He was made to strip naked and had to stand in front of all of the members of the group while they taunted him. Then they all took turns spanking him on his bare bottom. Then Carrie mentioned that two teenaged boys were regularly abused and finally excommunicated by the group, along with their mother. No one knows of their whereabouts.

I don't know where Carrie got this information, but I do know she is the only parent/grandparent who has any access to what is going on inside That Group because of her grandparent visitation rights. The little girl, by the way, is *my* granddaughter! I am horrified!

Ted and I are both shocked. How could this happen? Why doesn't Carrie call the police or protective services? Maybe she will. But will it be too late when she makes the call? Is there a statute of limitations here? I ran into this law a couple of years ago after I filed a police report regarding allegations of child abuse against my grandson. I never heard back from the police—not even a peep. Are the children victims of this law? How many other crimes perpetrated against children are never looked into because of this law? Have the Dark Ones gnawed their way into the laws of our land—into government offices and police departments and child protective agencies? I am devastated! Who will speak for these children? Who will protect them? Can no one stop the destroyers?

In the tale of Little Red Riding Hood, the wolf got in the house and ate up Little Red Riding Hood's grandmother. When the little girl discovered the wolf, she, too, was eaten up. A kindly woodcutter happened by, discovered the wolf, and cut it open, releasing the little girl and her grandmother.

Have my grandchildren already been eaten? Have all of the other children in That Group met the same fate? Has time run out for all of them? Is there no one who will cut this group open and save the children?

In the meantime, Ted and I have decided it would be best to find a new lawyer who practices closer to where my daughter lives and closer to where Ted works. I need to tell Rudy. I hate to let him go, but I think it would be best to do this, especially with me living so far away. I need to get people working for me who live and work in the same county. I need someone to rescue the children! Now!

Chapter 17

JANUARY 24, 2003

I spoke with my new lawyer, James, today. I feel somewhat encouraged. But then I have been encouraged before to no avail. I feel like Alice in Wonderland trying desperately to get help, to get back to the world I used to live in, but I can't figure out how. Things keep getting more bizarre, more abnormal. I can't seem to do anything to stop it from happening. Did anyone help Alice after she fell down the rabbit hole? I don't recall. I think she simply woke up while being chased by the Queen of Hearts. Will someone help me—please? Will someone wake me up? I don't want to be here!

Meanwhile, my new lawyer promised that he would read all of my journal writings and talk to Ted after he is finished. He also said that he may call the state's attorney's office regarding the case. He is not sure that the Grandparents' Visitation Rights Law is the way to go. He believes there might be another way. He needs to get all the information about the case before he decides to go forward with it.

And I ask, why is it so hard to proceed? To be fair, a lawyer needs to ponder all of the cases put before him and then decide to take them—or not. But all of the waiting on my end is interminable. At this point, I am emotionally spent. I don't know if I can do this for one more day! For one more hour! But I know that I have to.

> *Hear my cry, O God; listen to my prayer.*
> *From the ends of the earth I call to You,*
> *I call as my heart grows faint;*
> *Lead me to the rock that is higher than I.*
> *For you have been my refuge*
> *A strong tower against the foe.*
> *I long to dwell in your tent forever,*
> *And take refuge in the shelter of your*
> *wings*
> *—Psalm 61:1-4*

FEBRUARY 5, 2003

Ted to Sarah via email:

> I spoke with James this morning. He said he had not yet completed the journal—that it was longer than he had anticipated. He also said it looked like the main hope would be through a juvenile proceeding and that the Grandparents' Visitation Law didn't look possible. He told me that he would call me after he had read the entire journal and made a decision regarding the case.

FEBRUARY 6, 2003

Sarah to Ted via email:

Hi Ted. Thanks for your note. I wanted to remind you to please tell James about what you found out from Evin regarding the children/teens who have allegedly experienced child abuse at the hands of the adult members of That Group. If any of these incidents occurred in the last year this may help the case.

FEBRUARY 12, 2003

Sarah to Ted via email:

It seems like forever since I have heard from you! Do you know if anything is happening? I had asked James to try to get back with me within a couple of weeks to let me know if he is even remotely interested in taking the case and he said he would. It has now been three weeks and I am very weary. It is getting harder and harder for me to keep going. I suppose I am in some sort of slump right now. And I know that there is nothing you can do to hurry him along. Just let me know when you hear anything. I don't want to give up but I am just so tired. I know that the white rabbit cannot help me. Neither can the mad hatter . . . or the Jabberwocky . . . or Alice. I'm not even sure if God will help me . . .

FEBRUARY 13, 2003

That voice in the back of my mind, I heard it so clearly today. It said to me, "Don't give up now Sarah. You are getting close. Don't throw away all you have done! Concentrate. You can do this. I know you can. I know you. I know that you can fight through this. God is near to you. I know you can't see Him, but He is near. He weeps when you weep. He feels pain when you feel pain. Don't give up yet Sarah! And don't give up on God. He is as near to you as your own breath, and He is helping you. You just can't see it now. Keep praying to Him. He will rescue His children when the time is right. Don't give up until you are done! Fight, Sarah! Fight!"

FEBRUARY 14, 2003

Ted to Sarah via email:

> I'm sorry, but I thought I told you that I spoke with James last week and he said he was going to try to finish the journal over the weekend. I apologized to him for the journal being so long. I don't feel right rushing him when he is doing this on his own time. I'll check back with him soon. I suspect he will want to talk to the state's attorney after his review of the journal and that may also take some time. Please try to be patient. I know it is difficult.

FEBRUARY 18, 2003

Ted to Sarah via email:

I have talked with James. He has still not gotten completely through the journal; however, he said that while reading the journal he has been researching other ways you might be able to get some kind of contact with your grandchildren. He mentioned the possibility of a petition for guardianship through a probate action. Another option that no one else has thought of would be for you to file a petition for adoption of the children. With both of these petitions, you would need to allege and show proof that your daughter and/or son-in-law are incompetent. Lastly, you could go ahead and try to file a petition under the new Grandparents' Visitation Act. Actually James said you could file all three of these petitions at the same time. I know I suggested we wait until James has had the opportunity to digest everything and then to get his guidance on how to proceed with the investigation; and that is still my position. I also need to see the guidelines for incompetency. Even though this is taking a while, I think we are still moving forward.

Yes, I thought to myself, but we are moving forward *ever so slowly*! What if we get there too late? What if the Queen of Hearts and her soldiers come out from below to destroy the children before we get there? I need to fly to my garden: to think, to rest. I need to sit and wait for God. I will unfold my wings and fly away. Maybe God will be there this time. Maybe . . .

Chapter 18

I had another dream. I found myself caught up in a terrible storm. It was dark all around and I was alone. I did not know where I was, but I knew I needed to get to the light. I just did not know where to find it! Why was night always around me? Where was day? Why couldn't I find day? And if I found her, how could I capture her? Where was day?

I began to move forward, not knowing what the next step would bring—not knowing when a Dark Angel would appear or when a screeching owl would appear, with stretched out talons, razor sharp, ready to pluck me up and then throw me back onto the ground, dashing me to pieces.

Then I heard the voice from inside of me telling me that I needed to be brave. That I was not without help. But I saw nothing. I saw no one. No one at all.

FEBRUARY 23, 2003

Ted to Sarah via email:

> I spoke briefly with James today. He
> has read the journal and may have some
> other ideas about how to proceed. But
> you really need to talk with him. I think
> your idea of coming here and meeting
> with him is a good idea. Why don't you
> call him and make an appointment. I'll be
> happy to be present with you when you
> speak with James. I think we are starting
> to develop a lot of different options. It's
> encouraging!

MARCH 8, 2003

Today I will go to see Ted and James. I'm scared.
I don't know if I can do this. What if James decides
not to take the case? What then? Go back to square
one? I don't know if I have it in me to start over. The
journey is difficult enough without having to start
over again!

MARCH 9, 2003

James will take the case! He told Ted and me
that the moment we walked into his office he had a
revelation, and he has decided that we will file suit
against Jeze and That Group. We will not have to go
after a competency hearing for my daughter. We do
not need to seek guardianship of the children. We
will not seek grandparent visitation rights. This is

all good news—at least I think it is. But I don't want to get my hopes up too high.

> *"O that you would tear open the*
> *heavens and come down,*
> *So that the mountains would quake at*
> *your presence—*
> *As when fire kindles brushwood and the*
> *fire causes water to boil—to make your*
> *name known to your adversaries,*
> *So that nations might tremble at your*
> *presence!*
> *When you did awesome deeds that we*
> *did not expect,*
> *You came down, the mountains quaked*
> *at your presence.*
> *From ages past no one has heard, no*
> *ear has perceived,*
> *No eye has seen any God besides you,*
> *who works for those who wait for him."*
> *—Isaiah 64:1-4*

MARCH 21, 2003

Ted to Sarah via email:

> I spoke with James last week. He received your check. He will be working on the complaint this week and once he gets a rough draft together, he will send a copy to me. Once I have the complaint, I will want to start talking with other people who have been involved in That Group.

Over the next few months, Ted, James, and I emailed and phoned each other numerous times. James wrote and rewrote many drafts of the complaint, trying to get the best document possible from a legal point of view so the judge assigned to the case would sit up and take notice.

And more and more I felt like we were all characters from a dream following a narrow road, through forests and fields, stumbling over all manner of obstacles in the forms of legal documents, lawyers, judges, police, uncooperative witnesses, Dark Ones, and a Dark Angel named Jezebelle. With each passing day, my heart yearned for sanity, for calm, and for peace.

> *I wait, Lord. The children wait, Lord. We all wait for your appearing, Lord. Come, Lord Jesus. Come quickly. Cast out the darkness. Illuminate Your world. Bring us peace.*

In June of 2003, Ted began emailing me concerning my health. He warned me that litigation would be very stressful and wondered if I really want to do battle. He wrote that the witnesses he had interviewed were "real unusual people" and wondered if any of them would be of any help at all. He also warned that I would be attacked by the defense attorney and that my credibility might be questioned. He also told me that he had been an investigator for 31 years and that my case is one of the most difficult and strange cases he has ever worked on.

Sarah to Ted via email:

I know what we are dealing with more than anybody else. I know what Jeze is capable of, and I know she could destroy me if I am not careful. She is a very dangerous woman. Remember that one of her previous members told me that at one point after leaving That Group, he was afraid for his life. He also told me that there were many 'death prayers' and curses regarding me and my husband sent to God knows where, hell maybe? Jeze definitely wants us dead.

Having said all that, I do believe that the complaint is a long shot, and I do not want to commit suicide. But I am willing to take the risk if I can be reasonably assured that some former members of this group will testify as to how Jeze manipulated, controlled, and in general, tried to destroy their lives by causing great mental pain, and/or physical pain, alienation from their family members, etc. by threats, and punishments, both physical and mental.

It is vital that some of these people testify. I probably don't have a chance of winning without the corroboration of these people. So that is where I am. I have enclosed a rather lengthy list of people who might be willing to stand up in court and tell the truth. Please let me know what you think about interviewing these people.

JUNE 17, 2003

I talked to Ted today. He is interviewing some of the people on the list I sent to him. He said he is learning all kinds of interesting things! First of all Ted, went to see Evin again and while he was with him, in walked David, a former member of That Group. David told Ted that he wants to talk and then set up an appointment with him for the following week.

Evin, on the other hand, was somewhat reserved and guarded. Much more so than the last time Ted spoke with him. I would guess that Evin is afraid of Jeze! Evin did say that Jeze is very manipulative and uses others to do her work. He also explained that while Rob was a member of the group, Rob and his wife were ordered to break up. It was a rule that all members had to separate themselves from anyone who was deemed ungodly or unclean.

Ted also went to see Rob, and Rob had much to say. Among other things, Rob said that Annie was forced to sever all relationships with her extended family. She was forced to make a choice between her extended family and her husband and child. She chose her husband and child. (I would have, too.)

Rob said that Annie was very upset about having to sever her relationship with her extended family members—especially with me—her mother. She was at odds with Jeze for quite some time after that. Rob feels that deep down she still loves me; however, he is worried that too much time has passed at this point, and that she is in too deep and can no longer stand up for herself.

Ted told me that he had also interviewed a man named Will, but said that the interview was not very helpful. Ted spoke to several people who said that they did not want to get involved. Not surprising. In his interviewing, Ted also found out that Annie had lost a baby about 3 months ago. The baby was born with the cord wrapped around its neck. How sad that Annie has had to endure so much pain.

Most important of all, Rob told Ted that he was in Jeze's presence when she told Bret that Annie must sever all relationships with Sarah and Al because they were "ungodly and unclean." Rob was also with Bret and Annie when Bret told Annie what she had to do.

This is huge! We finally have a witness who can tell exactly why and when Annie had to cut off relationships with her family!

JUNE 19, 2003

Sarah to Ted via email:

> I am happy that you have interviewed so many people. I want to move ahead with the complaint. Jeze should not be able to get away with hurting so many people. I am having a very hard time thinking about Annie and the baby she lost. She has to be in agony. I am so sad that I cannot be there for her. Anyway, I would like to go full steam ahead with the complaint. I want to see my daughter. I want to see my grandchildren. I want to see Bret, too, even though I am mad at him. Please, Ted, do whatever you have to do. I am ready for the battle! I will do whatever it takes to free my daughter, her husband, and their children!

JUNE 23, 2003

Ted to Sarah via email:

> I met with David, a former member of That Group, yesterday and talked with him for quite a while. He's a nice kid, but he left the original church before Jeze and her followers broke off to form a new

church. He has some information about Jeze being controlling and manipulative, but the information may not be strong enough for your case. He told me a story about being confronted by Jeze and a few of her followers. Apparently they were upset with him because he was associating with someone they did not approve of.

I also called Leah and spoke with both her and her husband. She is really 'out there'! She babbled on and on about Jeze and That Group in general. She believes that the group has had a terrible effect on her and her extended family. They want to meet with me and their son and daughter-in-law in their home. I am planning on meeting with them next week.

There are some really screwed up people in this case—and we know who screwed them up. It's really sad. Actually, it's criminal! I don't know what kinds of witnesses any of them will make. I'm a little afraid that most of them are not going to know things that would be legally relevant or admissible. But, I'll keep talking to people. I want to talk to Katie K. next week.

JUNE 25, 2003

Sarah to Ted via email:

Keep talking, Ted! Listen very carefully to what they have to say. Yes, Leah is 'out there.' Perhaps she has had a breakdown of some kind? Please listen very carefully to all the people I have suggested that you interview. And yes, what has happened to many of these people is criminal. Perhaps we will be able to find some justice for at least some of them, and some peace. I know I'm asking a lot of you—perhaps setting you up for a dangerous situation. I believe that Jeze and her minions are capable of just about anything.

JUNE 30, 2003

Ted to Sarah via email:

I am hoping to talk with Katie K. next week. Apparently she has two sons who were badly treated by the leaders of That Group. She could be a world of information. I also have a message from Grayson to call him next week. I won't go into detail, but the more people I talk to, the crazier this thing gets!

JULY 12, 2003

Ted called me this afternoon. He told me he has spoken with Katie K., and that she was a fountain of information. One of the things she told Ted was that Jeze turned her against her mother, but not against her father. Her mother is a Christian; her father is not.

This is the same scenario that I experienced! Jeze, Annie, and all the rest of them turned against me and Al, who are both practicing Christians, but not against

Annie's biological father and stepmother who don't practice anything. Is Jeze that afraid of Christians? It appears as if she is—about as afraid as a vampire is of daylight, or the wicked witch of water!

Katie told Ted that she was "booted" out of That Group, while her two sons stayed—at least for a time. Consequently her sons turned totally against her. They still lived in the same house with their mother, but they never spoke to her. She said that she drove them to school every morning and they never uttered a single word to her as if she did not exist. Then she explained to Ted that she and her boys have recently reconciled and that the boys are out of That Group. Katie does not want Ted to interview the boys at this time, however, as they are too "raw." She believes that the group really messed them up. One of her boys is in college and the other one is in high school. Finally, Katie told Ted that she would be willing to talk more at a later time.

Chapter 19

MID-JULY, 2003

I have been dreaming of Annie again. Night after night I dream of her. She appears to be distraught—a mess—physically as well as emotionally. She wants to come home. She needs help with her children, and she can't do it anymore! She is living a nightmare.

I pray God will protect me and my entire family (including Annie, Bret, and their children)! Evil is lurking very near to me; hell's demons are furious with me! Am I getting too close to the truth? Perhaps the demons are trying to frighten me by playing with my mind. It is working. At times I am absolutely terrified! I emailed Ted yesterday. I did not tell him about the dreams and nightmares I have been having.

Ted has been able to speak to a number of potential witnesses. Rob told him that he would be willing to testify in court. Katie K. also said that she was willing to testify. Ted has not met with Grayson yet, but I believe he would also be willing to testify, as well as Detective Charles. But Ted has warned me that we need to go about it all very carefully. He does not want to offend—or frighten away—any potential witnesses! Rob could be our most important witness.

Ted told me that Rob verified the conversations he overheard when Jeze told Bret that Annie must break all ties with her mother. Ted may take some kind of formal written statement from Rob that could possibly be attached to our complaint. No wonder the demons are so furious with me! I am treading in dangerous waters, as is Ted. I need to pray for Ted's protection, and for our lawyer's protection, as well as all who are involved in this strange case.

JULY 25, 2003

I woke up very disturbed and very sad. I dreamed that Annie tried to take her own life. I went to her and took her in my arms. She was so small—so fragile—so lifeless—so sad. She appeared to be grateful that I had come. Hang on Annie! I'm trying to come to you! Know that I love you—don't give up! Don't quit until it is done! But I don't know how to get to Annie.

Where is hope? Where is justice? Are You out there God? Can You hear me? Or Not? Do You exist or are You just a figment of my imagination?

AUGUST 1, 2003

What a day! I met with Ted and Katie K. Katie and I bonded immediately. She told me many things, verifying all that I had already written down in my journals. She said That Group is a cult and that much abuse is going on. She said that Jeze is at the center of everything—she controls everything and deceives everyone.

Katie told me that when Rory was 4 or 5 years old, he was punished for some small infraction. Jeze, her husband Jeb, Annie and Bret, and Ray (Bret's brother) and his wife Theresa, made Rory lie down on the floor face up. Then they all circled around him and around and around him they moved—taunting him, shaming him, and trying to get him to cry, to break!

What kinds of monsters have these people turned into? Certainly the Annie and Bret I once knew and loved are not these monster creatures that Katie K. describes! Then Katie K. volunteered even more information:

> All of Jeze's followers had to pull away from their families of origin.
>
> When a former member's mother was dying, her sons, who were members of That Group, were not allowed to visit her. When she died, they were not allowed to attend her funeral.
>
> Katie believes that all of Jeze's followers are oppressed and that all are mistreated—physically, mentally, emotionally, and spiritually—both adults and children. They are all prisoners inside That Group. They just don't know it.
>
> Katie heard the leaders of That Group send curses of death upon Sarah and Al.
>
> Katie stated that the group caused her divorce.
>
> Jeze told one of her followers that her mother and father were filled with demons and her grandmother was in hell.

> Jeze and her minions love to intimidate others by circling around them, taunting them.

Why is this cult allowed to exist? Who will stop it? Who will rescue the children? Who?

AUGUST 9, 2003

My lawyer is getting ready to file the complaint. I don't know how I feel about it. This could be the end of That Group, or it could be the end of me. This whole legal endeavor may be a waste of time and money. The end result could be more damaging than what has already transpired. More people could get hurt. The damage could be irretrievable. What should I do? I could stop it all with one phone call. But then what would happen to the children? Would they forever be imprisoned? But am I foolish and vain thinking that I might be able to help them? Am I absolutely certain that I am sane? Am I certain that the children are real? Am I certain about anything? Am I certain that anything in my life is real? Do I live in the same dimension—in the same timeframe as other people? Who can help me? Who can tell me what to do?

AUGUST 10, 2003

Ted to Sarah via email:

> I met with James this morning, and we reviewed all of my notes of the various conversations/interviews I have had from some of the main witnesses for the case.

We also discussed the complaint. James thinks that he may amend the complaint based on the new information I gave him.

Actually James mainly sat and shook his head in disbelief while I went over all the notes. He told me that even if he needs to make some changes, the complaint should be ready to file at the end of this week.

When James is finished, he will want you to review the complaint and then give him the green light to file it. It is possible that I may be the one to serve the summons and complaint on Jeze. That should be interesting! I don't know how long it will take the court to issue the summons, but I will let you know when it is ready to be served and when it actually does get served! I am also lining up a reporter from the local newspaper to do some kind of an article on this lawsuit once it gets filed. If an article does appear about the lawsuit, I really think we may bring some people out of the woodwork that have had some kind of contact with Jeze or That Group— people who might be willing to speak with me!

AUGUST 16, 2003

I feel like I am on the brink of something. I'm just not sure what it is.

AUGUST 21, 2003

I received a copy of the new and revised complaint today. Ted and I discussed it over the phone. Hopefully this revised version will be filed this week. But why do I use the word 'hopefully'? I don't know if I am hopeful that any of this will be hopeful? What exactly am I hopeful for? That I can turn back the clock? That it has all been just a bad dream and I am about to wake up? That my daughter, son-in-law, and grandson will walk through my doorway as if nothing has happened? What exactly is it that I am hoping for? I don't know. I just don't know. What I do know is this: Nothing will ever be the same again. *How can I survive this new life, God?*

AUGUST 22, 2003

Ted to Sarah via email:

> I spoke with James today and he has dictated the changes in the complaint and I think it should be done tomorrow. I'll send you a copy as soon as I get it. I will then want to talk with you again before it gets filed. I also suggest you call and talk to James before this lawsuit gets started. Ask James any questions you can think of. I want you to be sure of everything. The more I think about it, the more convinced I am that it is the right thing to do.

I, Sarah, wish I could be so convinced that we are doing the right thing, but I am not convinced. I am frightened. I am sick to my stomach. My doubts could fill up an entire ocean. This is all about my daughter. How can I do this? How can I not? This is an impossible situation! Who is the bad guy here? Is it I?

I have to believe that God is in control here. But is He? Is God really in control of this situation—or anything else for that matter?

I don't get it, God! Where are You? I am exhausted! I can't do this anymore! I can't think about it anymore! I'm done! Have it Your way, Lord, but don't abandon them! If You want someone banished from Your Light, take me!

Now I lay them down to sleep.
I pray Thee Lord their souls to keep.
If they should die before they wake,
I pray Thee Lord, their souls to take!

AUGUST 23, 2003

I received a copy of the complaint today. I read it, and I don't even know what to think about it. My mind is numb.

AUGUST 24, 2003

Ted to Sarah via email:

> Call me with any other ideas you might have about the complaint. Even though it can be amended at a later date, I want to make it as complete as possible at the time of filing. We are going to take our best shot right now at the witch and her little cult.

AUGUST 25, 2003

I tried to reach James by phone today but was unsuccessful.

AUGUST 31, 2003

Sarah to Ted via email:

> Do you have any idea why the complaint has not yet been filed? I have called James on numerous occasions but have not been able to speak with him. I asked his secretary to call me when the complaint is filed. She keeps telling me "It will be filed today!" It has not been filed. I have stopped calling his office because I don't want to be a pest. Do you know what is going on? The wait is excruciating for me! I just want to get on with it and get the filing over with. Let me know when you hear anything please.

AUGUST 31, 2003

Ted to Sarah via email:

I apologize that James has not communicated with you. I called his secretary and she said James gave her your file and a dictation tape yesterday. She has not yet gotten to this tape, but will today. James must have made some additional changes. He told his secretary that he wanted me to look at this next draft of the complaint before it gets filed. I will look at it as soon as it gets done and then call you. James is gone until next Tuesday, but his secretary would be able to file the complaint with the circuit clerk's office. Hang in there. We'll get this rolling soon.

SEPTEMBER 1, 2003

Ted to Sarah via email:

We will need to wait to file the complaint as James is out of the office until next week. There seems to be a question about the proper way to serve the complaint. Here's the reason for the slight delay: That Group is a state corporation. The way a corporation must be served is that the process has to be served on an officer or registered agent of the corporation. The only person listed as an officer for the corporation is Ray, and he is listed as the registered agent as well. No one else is listed as an officer, though, I would bet that Jeze is probably the president of the corporation. However, since she is not listed, Ray would have to be served and Jeze would be served individually since she is a named defendant.

The address for the registered agent (Ray) is Jeze's address. Usually the registered address is a business or home address of the registered agent, but not this time. I assume Ray can be served at his own residence, but we need to ask James to be sure. This is a minor glitch, but we want to make sure that everything gets done properly. I ran a trace on Ray to get his exact home address.

SEPTEMBER 9, 2003

The complaint was filed yesterday—finally! Ted said he liked the judge assigned to the case, so that is good. Jeze and Ray will be served sometime next week.

SEPTEMBER 19, 2003

I haven't heard from anyone about anything since September 9th.

Is there anyone out there? Anyone at all? And what about You God? Surely You are out there. Aren't You? Give me a sign, God. I so desperately need a sign that everything will be ok. I need to know that You are with me. I need an answer!

Shall I sit in my garden today? Is that where I will

find You, God? Perhaps behind my Box of Memories? Or my Box of tears?

SEPTEMBER 30, 2003

I spoke with Ted today. He told me that the summons had been served on the 13th. I also received a letter from James today. He suggested that I get my journals, my correspondence, my pictures, etc., all organized. Our court date has been set for April, 2004.

Are we going forward then, God? Is this it? Are You with me? I am so afraid! What if this all backfires? What if I have made everything up? What if I am, indeed, insane? The worlds I live in are so different from everyone else's world! What if no one believes my story?

I need You, God! Please let me know that You are near to me.

OCTOBER 25, 2003

I dreamed about Annie last night. She was older, reserved, and unemotional. She came to see me, and we talked at length. Then she went home to her "other life." I was not allowed to go with her; I was not allowed to enter her "other life." She made it very clear that any relationship with me would not happen in her "other life." She will never be my daughter again.

Dear God, give me the strength to go on! Tell me what to do! Work through me! I cannot do anything without You!

DECEMBER 5, 2003

I received a phone call from Leah today. Her kids and grandkids are home! They left That Group and they all just walked into her life again—on Thanksgiving Day! They just showed up—unannounced! I am so happy for her.

When will it be my turn, God? When will my kids and grandkids come home? How can I endure this torture? It is too much, dear Lord. It is just too much.

DECEMBER 7, 2003

I am doing what I have been doing for the past 7 years. Waiting. Waiting for something to happen. Waiting for *God* to make something happen! How long, Lord? How long?

DECEMBER 23, 2003

Sarah to Ted via email:

I am happy that our case continues to move forward, albeit very slowly. A week or so ago you told me that the 'other side' has now retained a powerful lawyer in town.

You also told me that he does not want to make any deals with me regarding this case. I don't think he has any idea whatsoever as to what this case is really all about. Nor does he have any idea about all of the information we have, or all of the potential witnesses we have. Al and I have talked about 'deal making,' and we have decided that we do not want to make any deals. We want this case to go to trial. The case is far more than what has happened to my daughter. It is about all of the people Jeze has hurt—including many innocent children. Jeze needs to be exposed for the deceiver she is. How else can this horrible group be dismantled? There is no other way. Have a blessed Christmas. Talk to you soon!

I am reminded of the story of Hansel and Gretel. Hungry and lost in the woods one day, the brother and sister stumbled upon a gingerbread house made up of all kinds of good things to eat. And so they ate of it. Then, much to their surprise, they discovered that a kindly lady lived inside the house and that she was all too happy to continue to feed them until they returned home.

Towards the end of this tale, however, this kindly lady is exposed for who she really is—a cruel witch. And her goal is to fatten up the children and then eat them! Thank heavens, before the story ends, the kindly lady is exposed and the children are able to push her into the oven where she stays forever after.

Jeze needs to be put away *forever,* too—in a place where she will *never again* be able to hurt any children.

JANUARY, 2004

Sarah to Ted via email:

> Are you out there, Ted? I haven't heard from you in some time and the case is supposed to be filed tomorrow. Is this still going to happen? At times you are the only lifeline to my sanity—where are you? Please tell me what, if anything, is going on.

JANUARY 13, 2004

Ted to Sarah via email:

> Sorry, but I have three trials starting Tuesday, in three different counties, and a murder case hearing this morning that has consumed much of my time. My work is sometimes very overwhelming and stressful with everyone wanting, or needing, things done all at the same time. This is one of those times for me and I can't always get back to you right away.
>
> I've skimmed through all of the materials you have left for me and have discussed your case with James. He said that he has everything he needs to complete the revised filing. This process is going to take some time, so please try to be patient. I will keep you advised as well as I can as to what is going on.

JANUARY 13, 2004

Sarah to Ted via email:

> Thanks for getting back with me Ted. I will try my best to be patient.

LATE AFTERNOON, JANUARY 13, 2004

Ted to Sarah via email:

> My murder case went pretty well and one of my out-of-county cases got continued. Some of my problematic situations seem to have pretty much resolved themselves today.

I will try to send you a more detailed email in the next couple of days, but I wanted you to know that I talked to James again and he said his deadline for the revised filings on your case was extended for another week, so it is not due until January 20th. James said that your journal and the other materials were interesting, but he did not believe that any of it would be of any benefit. I know you are anxious about this case, but I don't think we will know anything for quite some time. I know you are trying to be patient, and I appreciate that.

JANUARY 30, 2004
Ted to Sarah via email:

James filed and the lawyer for the other side has responded to James' revised filing of your case. I am attaching a copy of James' response to the defendant's motions. I think he did a really good job.

FEBRUARY 3, 2004
Ted to Sarah via email:

I would like you to think about and maybe list your thoughts on the conditions you would want for any type of visitation with your grandchildren.

FEBRUARY 3, 2004

Sarah to Ted via email:

Does Jeze's lawyer believe that we have a good case? Is that why James wants me to list my thoughts about possible visitation rights? I don't know what is going on. I thought we were not going to make any deals. Does Jeze's lawyer want to make a deal of some kind? I don't want to do anything until I know what is going on. I will wait patiently until someone tells me what is going on.

FEBRUARY 7, 2004

Sarah to Ted via email:

Al and I want to thank both you and James for all of your efforts on the case to date. We hope that James can come up with something that will have a precedent in our state's case law. Something that will make the judge feel okay about taking it to trial. I just need to say now, that if the judge does not determine that the case has enough merit to go to trial, we do not know whether or not we want to appeal. We know that you and James are doing your best to get this case heard, but 'best' is not always enough. Let's see what happens.

MARCH 17, 2004

Sarah to Ted via email:

> I have not heard anything from James for quite some time. Perhaps he has had to redo the complaint, again? I grow more impatient by the day. (My problem not yours). Perhaps there is nothing more that can be done. Perhaps it is time to let the suit go? I have a bad feeling that things are not going to work out.

MARCH 18, 2004

Ted to Sarah via email:

> Don't give up the ship yet! I think James has been gone and he has also been dealing with his wife's health issues. Call me around the middle of next week and we can talk.

APRIL 3, 2004

Sarah to Ted via email:

> I have not heard from James for weeks. I have stopped calling his office because his secretary seems to be tired of me calling. I can hear it in her voice! I think James was to go before the judge last week but I am not sure. No communication. I fear that the case will be—or has already been—dismissed by the judge. Too much silence. I feel as if I may be moving into the stage of 'acceptance,' at least as far as anything

legal getting done. There is no other place for me to go.

I don't know if a relationship between us and Annie and her husband and children will ever be possible. Too much time has gone by. And this whole lawsuit is much bigger than merely visitation rights at this point. It's about exposing Jeze and That Group to the world. It's about putting together shattered souls. It's about saving lives!

APRIL 5, 2004

Ted to Sarah via email:

I found out that the deadline for James to file an amended complaint on That Group's lawyer's attempted dismissal of your case was yesterday. This was not an argument before the judge but a written response. I've attached James' amended complaint. I don't know how long it will be before the judge will rule on this response. This all means that your case was brought before a judge and the lawyer for the 'other side' moved to dismiss it. Then the judge gave James time to amend the complaint. Sorry this is taking so long.

MAY 18, 2004

Sarah to Ted via email:

Hi Ted. We have not communicated for a long time. James is still forging ahead on the case. I don't have a lot of hope, but I do have more hope than I did a couple of months ago. Otherwise I would not have sent him more dollars to move forward with the case! He did write me a letter and told me he is reasonably 'encouraged' that the judge will rule in my favor.

I wish everything would get cleared up soon—one way or another. This whole thing has just crippled my life! Please call me if you hear anything important about the case.

MAY 19, 2004

Ted to Sarah via email:

Sorry I have not been in contact with you lately. As usual, I have been busy dealing with criminals and attorneys (can't always tell them apart). I've been involved in three murder cases, one of which is in trial this week.

Part of the reason I have not been in touch is because there is nothing new to report about your case. It's a matter of waiting to see what the judge rules. Anyway, hoping the right thing happens with your case.

LATE SPRING, 2004

It seems to be over at this point. There is one more court hearing before the judge, but it will take a miracle for him to move our case forward. Perhaps it is time to end our legal battle. We could go on, we could appeal—but what would be the point? To face more disappointment? More grief? More financial drain?

Has it all been an elaborate hoax? From the Evil One himself? Has it been merely a trap set up to destroy my family and me? If this is the case, then the Evil One has won. The Prince of Darkness has handily won.

I am done. I no longer have the energy or the will to fight. I must come to terms with the loss of my daughter, my son-in-law, and my grandchildren. They are no longer in my life. All the doors are closing. Darkness hovers all around. I can see no light at all.

God seems to have abandoned us all. Why? I don't know. I will never know. I have no hope—no hope at all. I gave it all I had, but God chose not to answer my prayers. I will never know why. Now I need to choose to continue to believe. Or not. The choice is mine.

OCTOBER 2, 2004

It is over—officially over! The judge dismissed our case! I am done with everything! Are You out there God? Should I be done with You too? You seem to be done with me. Forgive me, God, but I don't feel that You are here with my family and me at all!

And all the King's horses, and all the king's men, could not put Humpty together again. And no one can put me together again either.

MAY, 2005

I had a dream last night about Annie and Rory (who was 17 in the dream and about to graduate from high school). Annie and I cried and cried and cried together for all the lost years. The dream was so real. Was it perhaps a sign from God? Or just a dream.

Hope left me months ago. For me, hope resides only in fairy tales and dreams, not in the real world. At least not in *my* worlds.

Restore my hope, God! Restore in me a new heart! I am so lost!

I will fly to my garden today; and I will sit there and wait. Surely God will come. I will sit and wait for Him . . .

Chapter 20

LETTERS TO ANNIE

Dear Annie,

I wish you could know how much I love you—and Bret and little Rory. I wish you knew how much I have fought for you. But it is over. You are all gone from our sight—forever. But, Dear Heart, you will never be gone from my heart, and from my thoughts and prayers. You will never be gone from my soul. My soul weeps for you. My soul will always hunger for you.

There is so much I wish to tell you, Annie. How I love you! How I miss you! How I wish we had been closer as a family, as mother and daughter. Perhaps then, none of this would have happened.

I remember your beginning years so clearly. You were happiest when I carried you close to me. I can still feel your little body nestled against my chest. I can still smell your baby scent and feel your fuzzy little head of hair against my cheek. I carried you with me everywhere. As a matter of fact, your feet barely hit the ground until you were five and needed to go to kindergarten. That was so traumatic! According to your teachers, you would cry and cry for me every day, all through kindergarten and halfway through first grade. None of us knew why. We just dealt with it as best as we could. Perhaps I should have kept you back a year—you were so young—a late summer baby—barely five when you started school. Perhaps I should have done many things differently.

You spent a lot of time crying during your growing up years, and I never figured out why. Why were you so unhappy? Was something bothering you that you could not explain to me? Did you think I didn't love you?

Did you think your dad didn't love you? We both loved you dearly. Did you not know it? Did we not love you enough? Were we unable to give you all that you needed? But we can't undo what was or wasn't done. It just was. And now it is. And you have been gone for a long, long time. Perhaps you will be forever. How could we have failed you that much?

Dear Annie,
Precious little baby of mine,
Round and soft and silky,
Hair damp from crying,
Tiny hands balled into fists.

Eyes wet,
With tiny tears.
What are you trying to tell me?
Do you hurt inside?
Are you cold?
Are you too warm?
Do you not know how much I love you?
What is it?
What are you trying to tell me?
If only I could figure it out!
I am your mother!
I should be able,
To figure it out!
But I cannot
Figure it out.
No one can.
Forgive me little child of mine,
For you are still my child.
And you are still hurting.
Still crying
On the inside.
Where no one can see.
So no one can know.
But I know.
I am still your mother.
And,
You are still my child.
You will always be my child,
Even though you are grown.
Even when you are old.
And I will always be trying,
To figure it all out.

Dear Annie,
I wonder what you look like.
It has been such a long time.
Do your eyes still flash with intensity?
Or are they dull now—
With worry and fatigue—
And sadness.
How many children do you have now?
Four? Five? Six?
I wish I knew all of their names.
I wish I could see their faces.
I am so sorry that you lost one of them.
I grieve too.
He—or she—was my grandchild.
Do your children know that I exist?
Do you know how much I love you?
I want you to know that I am not angry
with you
About leaving us.
I was never angry with you.
I will never be angry with you.
It was not your fault.
It has never been your fault.
None of it.
I wish I could be with you.
I wish,
I could see your face.
Do you have tears there?

On your face?
Tears for the baby you lost?
Tears for me?
Tears for yourself?
Or,
Do you keep the tears deep inside,
In a very dark place.
If only I could reach out to you.
But I cannot.
Nor can you reach out to me.
It is what is.
And I can only sit and wonder,
What you look like.

Hush little baby,
Don't say a word.
Mama's going to buy you
A mocking bird.
And if that mocking bird don't sing,
Mama's going to buy you a diamond
ring.
And if that diamond ring don't shine . . .
—Some words from a children's nursery
rhyme

Dear Annie,
Spring has come.
It is the first Spring I have noticed
In a long time.
Spring has come.
I can see it, hear it, smell it.
And it is a mystery.
Why now?
For Spring is hope.
And I am without hope.
I am empty of it.
I am,
Empty.
And yet,
In my emptiness,
In the middle of my nothingness,
God is near.
I can hear God breathing.
I can feel His presence.
And nothing else matters.
Nothing.
God is with me;
And my soul is safe.
Spring has come.
And perhaps in time,
My tears,
Hidden in the dark,
Will spring forth,
And I will no longer,
Need to hold them back.
My tears will come,
In the remembering.
Not in the hoping,

But in the remembering.
Spring has come.
I wonder if you see it.
I wonder if you still have hope.
I wonder.
I wonder.
Do tears come for you??
In the remembering?
Do you ever think of me?
Do you imagine what I look like?
Can you remember the sound of my voice?

PART 4

Epilogue

EARLY SPRING, 2013

I saw my grandson, Rory, for a brief fifteen minutes. A friend told me he worked at a local restaurant, so Liz and I went together and we met him. Amazingly, he seemed fine. He was very polite and shook our hands and said he was glad to meet us. We got fifteen minutes of absorbing him. He has one more year of high school remaining. The dream I had of him a number of years ago came true—at least partially true. I got to see him! I didn't get to see his mom. But I got to see him! He is a big boy—tall at 6'5" and built like a football player. He's handsome; he looks like the perfect blend of his parents. He told us he had no knowledge of why his family cut off relationships with his grandparents and others. He has no knowledge of anything unpleasant during his early years.

For that, I am so thankful. He told us his parents and siblings were doing fine. All of the rest of his siblings are still being homeschooled. He explained that his two sisters had been enrolled in high school, but then his parents abruptly pulled them out. He didn't know why.

Liz cried in front of him; I did not. But we both gave him hugs when his break was finished and he had to get back to work. He left us his cellphone number before he went back to the kitchen.

We were in shock after we left the restaurant—stunned at what had just happened after so many years! It was like a dream! But we were cautious about what had taken place. We weren't sure what would happen next—with him—with us—with anything that had just happened.

We were right to be cautious. The next day I received a text from him. He said his parents had found out about our meeting. They told him he could not see or speak to us again while he lived under their roof. This did not surprise either Liz or me. We are bitterly disappointed, but not surprised. He will graduate next spring, hopefully move out of his home and go to college or work full time, or perhaps even join the military. Liz and I pray that things will be different then. That he will contact us. Start a relationship with us. But we can't know what the future will bring. And so we wait. And pray.

But I found myself angry with God! How could God allow us to meet him knowing that he would be almost immediately yanked away from us? Was this some kind of cruel cosmic joke at our expense?

By Christmas Eve, 2013, I was furious with God. I could barely get through Christmas Eve services. I did not want to believe in Him anymore! Then Christmas morning came and I asked myself if I could truly say

I did not want to believe in God anymore. If I decided to go that route, there would never be any hope. All would be darkness from birth to death, and death would have the final word. Death would bring the darkness that would last for an eternity. Is that what I really wanted?

Then the Lenten season came, and a few weeks before Easter—right in the middle of Monday night choir practice—I experienced an epic revelation. The biggest crisis in my life was not in the losing of my daughter, my son-in-law, and my grandchildren.

I realized I wasn't sure that I believed in God anymore! I wasn't even sure how long I had felt that way! I had been preaching and teaching for years. How many of those years had I been struggling with my faith?

Had I ever believed? I certainly wasn't acting like I had ever believed. Even worse—had I merely been *pretending* to believe? And I realized that I did not know the answers to any of these questions!

I realized the biggest crisis in my life was in the losing of my faith!

And so I prayed—right in the middle of the choir anthem we were practicing! Right then and there, as I was singing my alto part, in my place, in the choir loft! And as I was praying, our voices sang as I had never heard us sing before—it seemed to reach straight to heaven, joining a choir of angels singing with us! And all while we sang, I prayed, and I begged God to help me believe! I cried out to God to banish my unbelief! I begged God to help me give it up—the pain, the sorrow, the hurt, and anger! I asked God to help me to choose to believe! To restore my faith!

Renew my faith, Lord God! The faith you gave me as a child. The faith that carried me through my growing up years—and most of my adult years—before I lost it. Before the sky turned black. Before I put all my memories in the memory box and all my tears in the tear box. Lord, I want to believe! Take away my unbelief! Take away the Dark Angel that has nearly ruined my life—the Dark Angel that has been eating away at my soul! Tell the Prince of Darkness and his minions to flee from me! I don't want the darkness to win! I don't want the darkness to overcome the Light!

Help me to surrender my life to You. To trust that You, ultimately, are in control of the universe and everything in it! Help me to be brave enough to face the Dark Ones that may yet storm the gate. To be strong enough, with Your help, to tell them to flee. To tell them that You are by my side and that You are my fortress and that they cannot enter through the gate of that fortress! Why did I ever think that all the king's horses and all the king's men could put us all together again! No earthly army can put us together again without You, God! No army in the whole wide world! No army save Your Army, God! Your Army of Angels of Light! With Jesus Christ, the Light of the World, as their Leader!

A mighty fortress is our God,
a sword and shield victorious;
He breaks the cruel oppressor's rod,
and wins salvation glorious.
The old satanic foe,
has sworn to work us woe!
With craft and dreadful might,
he arms himself to fight.
On earth he has no equal.
—From A Mighty Fortress Is Our God
By Martin Luther (1483-1546)

Lord God, prepare me for battle. I can't give up until it is done. I need to fight for my daughter. I need to fight for my grandchildren. I need to fight for many who are caught up by the Dark Ones. I can do all things with You by my side. Work through me, Lord. And work through all others who want to be warriors for You. Work through ALL of us so that we might be a part of your Army of Light and defeat the Dark Ones—for good.

How could I have thought You abandoned us? You never abandoned any of us! I just had to finish my story first and then look back at the whole story from start to finish. Not in pieces or parts or at different times—but as a whole. You have never left my side. You never left any of us! Your Amy of Light has been battling against the Dark Ones and their leader, the Prince of Darkness all along! How could I have been so blind?

And that 15 minutes I experienced with my

grandson? That was no cosmic joke. You provided me with those minutes so I could hear my grandson tell me that his family is doing okay. You spoke through my grandson! They are all safe! The Darkness has not completely taken over their lives! You have been and still are, with them!

In my anger at You I cried out, "Unless I see I will not believe!"

Today I cry out boldly, "My Lord and my God!" just as the disciple Thomas cried out when he saw his Lord's hands and feet and the scars in them where the nails had been. "Then Jesus told him, 'Because you have seen me, you have believed; blessed are those who have not seen and yet have believed" (John 20:29).

I am ready, God. I am ready to fight, to engage in battle once more with You by my side—with Your Army of Warriors both earthly and heavenly by my side! Let the battle begin!

Stand firm then, with the belt of truth buckled around your waist, with the breastplate of righteousness in place, and with your feet fitted with the readiness that comes from the gospel of peace. Take up the shield of faith, with which you can extinguish all the flaming arrows of the evil one. Take the helmet of salvation and the sword of the spirit, which is the word of God (Ephesians 6:14-17).

ONE YEAR LATER

2014

They are all out! I have just received the news! They are all out! My daughter still wants nothing to do with us, but they are out, and that is what is important. They are out from under the influence of the Dark Angel! Thanks be to God! We fought the battle and we won!

The Dark Angel thought she had taken everything.

She took away my work, my family, my peace, my sanity.

She took away my mornings and my nights.

She took away hope.

She took away tears that fall.

She took away light.

But she did not take away my soul.

She did not take away my faith.

And she did not,

Take away God.

I have everything that I need.

Continue to keep them safe, Lord. Until we meet again . . .

Now I lay them down to sleep,

I pray thee Lord their souls to keep.

And if they die before they wake,

I pray thee Lord their souls to take.

And the story continues to unfold . . .

For more information about
Sarah Elizabeth Rose
&

Ordinarily Sarah
please contact:
ordinarilysarah@gmail.com

For more information about
INKSWIFT
please visit:

www.inkswift.com

Over the years of living out her peculiar story of battling dark forces, Sarah discovered that she had been placed on an Enemy List created by a "church that wasn't really a church." She also discovered that for most of those years, she had the "honor" of being Enemy #1!

What did it mean to be Enemy #1? It meant that the leadership of the "church that wasn't really a church" let all of its members know that Enemy #1 was evil, and needed to be avoided at all costs. It meant that the Enemy's family was also evil. It meant that the Enemy's daughter, a member of the "church that wasn't really a church," was constantly looked upon as coming from bad seed, and that her six children, in turn, also came from bad seed. It meant that the Enemy's daughter and six children endured regular punishments during "worship services" inside the "church that wasn't really a church," for the evil thoughts and the evil spirits that they carried inside their bodies.

Being Enemy #1 also meant that Sarah was cursed daily during "worship." It meant that Sarah became the subject of daily "Death Prayers" during "worship." It meant that the leadership of the "church that wasn't really a church" wanted Sarah dead. Alas, because of the dangerous situation Sarah found herself in over the years, she decided to use a pen name, (Sarah Elizabeth Rose), to keep her identity at least somewhat hidden from those who wanted to harm her. She also created an email address for Sarah Elizabeth Rose, enabling readers to contact her.

S.E.R.